idioStylez Publications Presents,

More Than a Friend:

The Official, Unofficial Love Story of Ari & Tee

By Shay Quinn

More Than a Friend: The Official, Unofficial Love Story of Ari & Tee

Text Copyright © 2017 Shay Quinn

All Rights Reserved

Dedication:

I would like to dedicate this book to my mother, and two sisters who have always encouraged me to write and never give up. To someone I consider a step-father who has pushed me to publish and lastly, to a special friend who supported me and stayed by my side when life got tough.

Thanks, and I love you all

Writing for Existence

Existence,

the state or fact of existing, being.

Continuance in being or life,

the fact that you matter, matters.

Noticed by few,

loved by a couple,

wanted by none,

yet respected by all.

Living through words etched on paper,

revealed after the life has left,

the last breath taken,

now everyone wonders.

Hope is now lost,

and forever is no more,

but yet more relevant now than ever before.

Life, living, thankful,

ink, paper,

eternal.

----> More Than a Friend <----

"Let your passion for wanting to live be the sole guide that keeps you from existing; the fact that you matter, matters"

Chapter 1

A lot of people live life simple-minded, having a basic mindset or way of thinking; foolish. Typically focused more on material things and trying to keep up with every fad, or live life through social media. That's where they exist. The women take their clothes off, taking pictures with only panties and bras on. Putting themselves out there usually posting "men ain't shit" or "all men are the same". They post more club pictures than pictures of them hanging out with their kids. All for 'Likes'! The men on there are usually flashing money, posting pictures of cars, trucks and bags of weed. They are usually the ones who are the fakest. The ones who grew up in the projects with roaches, eating mayonnaise sandwiches, and who came to school smelling like piss, moth balls and incense. They are the ones who never had authentic name-brand clothes or whose mothers were boosters and fucking dime bag dope boys; the lame ones who stayed posted at the park or corner stores and didn't take the time to actually get out there and get some real money. They had no personality and tried creating one based off what other people posted on Instagram or Facebook.

They thrived to be like everything they'd heard on the radio or had seen in a music video. They reinvented themselves and perpetrated to be better than what they really were. Most people now days *exist* and don't *live*. They simply are occupying space and time, being inanimate. They exist, which is necessary, but not sufficient for life. Some people begin life existing, or just being another statistic; another walking, talking being. When you exist, you are merely just present in life, and then you die. Some, but not all people get to a point in life where they start living, where they enter a more elaborate process.

Living involves a beginning, middle and end, all of which are ineluctable. It requires action and sparks emotions. You actually feel alive because it means to feel emotions like love, to receive love and to give love, to feel anger, happiness, passion, and excitement. Living is to have ambition, knowing what you want in life and obtaining it. It means to follow dreams and never stop knowing what you want and going for it. Hell, a rock exists but it doesn't live, or feel, or even breathe and think. It's simply there.

You have to decide what type of person you want to be. Everyone has to make that choice one day. Ari'Yonnah Marie Childers, on the other hand had made that decision long ago that she wanted to live because she'd never had the chance to. She'd had an okay start to life, living with her mom and dad in a nice home. It wasn't the biggest house on the block or the nicest, and it wasn't the smallest or shabbiest either, at least to her it wasn't. A three bedroom, one bathroom house in a middle-class neighborhood, not in the ghetto, but close enough to experience it a little, she was happy. Her mom had taste, so even though they weren't rich, their house still looked nice and looked like they had money. Their lawn was kept and the grass was green.

Ari's mom had style, and passed that down to her. Ari was content with her middle- class lifestyle. She had nice clothes and she stayed clean. Their house didn't have roaches, and it didn't have crystal vases either. Every morning Ari went to school with a full stomach because her mom always said, "you can never go to school hungry because you wouldn't focus if you had rumbling in yo tummy." She would tickle Ari's belly and she would laugh until she couldn't breathe. For lunch, she never had to eat the nasty food they served in the stinky cafeteria, and after school she always had a snack before her mom would sit down with her and do homework. Ari's mom was everything in her eyes. That was until she passed away.

Ari losing her mother was when she found herself just existing. She understood that probably would have been the time when most people started to live. But not Ari, that's when she started to just *exist*. Her father hated her and showed it by raising his hands to her every chance he got. When she lost her mother, she lost her will to live. The only person who made her want to live was Kyra, her best friend. She had been there through thick when Ari basically had no one. Kyra was the one who held her at night, sometimes after beatings, and kept her secret so she wouldn't be taken away.

Kyra Leslie was very pretty and always had been. Her dark-skinned complexion was flawless. She was very pretty to be so dark, some people would say, but that didn't faze her. She often turned heads even when they were younger. Having always had a head full of thick, jet black hair that fell right below her earlobe. She was a dime piece, even though she was skinny with small boobs and absolutely no ass, her face made up for that. She had undeniable beauty, dark skin and all. She had always been the one who knew and got along with everyone. She was someone who Ari considered to be *living*. Kyra and her mother had a good relationship, but she never knew her father. Kyra was her mother's favorite child and all her other siblings knew it. They were jealous of her and never had a relationship with her because of that. That was yet another reason Kyra and Ari were so close. Kyra had no one she could relate to and Ari had no one at all. That was until Ari met Tee, well Tommy was what most people called him, but not Ari.

Thomas Howard Anderson was Ari's best friend. He was the reason she considered herself *living* now. Very competent in every aspect of his life, Tommy was motivated, well- rounded and well-respected by everyone. To know Tommy was to love Tommy. He was very shrewd in his work endeavors, but very sincere when it involved family and close friends. Not only because of the position he was in, but because of the person he was, inside and out. Tommy and Ari were one and the same when it came to their personalities; white or black, no gray area. Their bond was not like most people's bonds. They had a relationship their own friends and family didn't understand. Tommy had been there for Ari and his family had accepted her as one of their own. They were connected in a way that scared Ari sometimes. Ari liked to believe she meant the world to him, just like he did to her. She was always open with males that she'd dated because she knew that most men were not too fond of having their woman so close to another man. She'd made it a point to let them know firsthand Tee would not be going anywhere and if he called she was going. She could do that because she knew he was the same with her. Ari believed that Tommy and her were more than friends. Their connection wasn't sexual or even a dating relationship, and she believed that's why they were how they were. Was it possible to be soulmates with someone and not date them? Well, that's how Ari felt she and Tee were, soulmates in universe type of a way. Ari and Tommy decided years ago, that they could never date and that it was best for them to remain friends before they lost that. Ari never wanted to get to a point where she hated him, or he hated her, and they couldn't be in the same room together and not acknowledge each other's presence. Tee was to Ari a one of a kind friend. They knew everything about each other inside and out. She trusted him and he trusted her. Ari felt untouchable whenever she was with Tee or near him. He held her down and she him. No bitch or no nigga could ever come in between them, Ari and Tee made sure of it.

Ari, before Tee, had a plain, very unostentatious upbringing; very ordinary and typical. Tee, on the other hand, was the total opposite. Born into money, he lived a lavish and dangerous lifestyle since day one. His family was well known for their dealings in narcotics, something like a cartel. They ran the spectrum of everything from marijuana to crack cocaine. Ari stayed in her own lane and tried to ignore everything that was going on around her. She didn't spend too much time in that specific part of his life for her own personal reasons, and because he never wanted her to be a part of that. Like most things, sometimes you can't keep some things separate. Every now and then things would come into play because of his lifestyle. Ari didn't ask questions, but she listened and paid attention. She learned a lot from Tee and the people in his Association, but she didn't let that change her or deter her from where she wanted to be. Ari felt as though she was the same Ari Childers that she had been before she'd met him. Still shy, quiet, and keeping to herself, Ari was just a little older and less naïve.

----> More Than a Friend <----

"A man is only as strong as his team, so go ahead and respect me cause ain't no way in hell I'ma let you disrespect me"

Chapter 2

Ari grew up remembering how her mother would always say, "Birds of a feather flock together." She didn't know if she believed that. Ari was so different from the people she ran with; the people she now considered family. Most of the ladies were confident and sure of themselves. They knew who they were, what they wanted and didn't mind expressing it. All of them were beautiful and had the attitudes to go with it. Ari, on the other hand, was a bit more reserved. She knew she was beautiful but didn't normally flaunt it. She stayed fly mainly because of the things Tee bought her, and from the money she received from the Uncles. Because she was a part of the family she received a monthly allowance also.

Finding herself using little to no make-up, she mainly rocked a natural beat face, to keep up with the other girls. It took only one night when Tee and Ari were chilling in his whip for her to change her perspective on wearing make-up. At the time his choice of vehicle was a black 2007 Dodge Charger. It was all-black with two royal blue fender hash racers stripes. He had 30-inch royal blue and black rims that had an intertwining design. The sound system made you feel as though you were at a live concert when he passed by. In the car, the bass beat against your back like one of them massage chairs at the nail shop. It was a muscle manly looking car that fit him perfectly and he loved it. Parked outside of Uncle Tevin's house, all the girls, Meka, Juicy, Kyra and Mia, were spread around it talking, and all their boyfriends, Mills, Justin, Danny and Chris were talking amongst themselves too. It was a hot summer night so all the neighbors were out and people were in the street playing ball. It was mostly black people in the neighborhood and they knew just about everyone.

"Why you got on all of that make-up shorty?" Tommy asked Ari, continuing to sip on the dark brown liquid in his cup.

She knew it was some type of alcohol, but he wouldn't let her drink any of it. He always said she'd have to wait to drink if she wanted to do it, but he would not condone it. The other boys wouldn't allow her to drink either if they had purchased drinks for the other girls. Tee always said "a woman shouldn't drink hard liquor, maybe some wine or something softer, that's socially acceptable." Ari ate up everything he said on most days, so she listened. Tommy was very smart and wasn't the average dope boy from the block. He was bred to be a man and being raised by his mother, father and uncles aged him. He had an old soul, but also very generational.

He continued, "I don't like you wearing all that make–up, you already cute and you don't need no extra!"

Tee paused and Ari repositioned herself so they could face each other. With the palm of his hand, he traced Ari's small yellow face, pulled her in and kissed her. Bashful, her eyes instinctively rested on her hands.

"Besides these older niggas be watching you and I don't wanna have to put one of them down for fuckin' wit my li'l mama."

She smiled but he didn't. He took another sip of his brown substance and she knew he was serious. Ari knew how he felt about her and when he said those words she knew he meant every one of them.

Tee was very protective of Ari and she loved that about him. He had been that way since day one. She often thought back, remembering the first time he ever went there with a nigga over her. She was freaked all the way out. It all started because of Kyra as always.

"Kyra, you ready to leave yet?" Ari asked Kyra as everybody started to get riled up outside of the house the party had just taken place in. The party had ended 30-minutes ago, and Kyra was still standing outside talking to this guy she had met during the party. Ari wasn't even supposed to be out and knew she would get in trouble if her dad found out.

"Yeah girl, hold up" Kyra said continuing to talk. She was leaned up against the guy's car, smiling ear-to-ear, dressed in a short mini-skirt you could tell she was trying to be sexy. She was definitely cute and rocking the

mini, but that was the furthest thing from Ari's mind, she was ready to go.

Ari sighed and continued to wait for her. Standing only a few feet away, Ari spotted Tommy and his group of friends by his car. They were cool but lived a bad lifestyle from what she'd heard over the past few weeks when a few people found out they were cool. She didn't know if they were jealous or really looking out for her best interest. All she knew was he was always nice to her and had even bought her a cell phone.

"Hi Tee" Ari greeted walking over to kill time while she waited for Kyra.

"What's up ma?" he said stepping out his 85' Cutlass Supreme to talk to her. It was olive green with an ivory interior. He loved his Cutty and only brought it out during the summer. It had 26-inch rims and they were clean, shining even though it was dark out. You could tell he spent a lot of money on it.

"Nothin' was waiting for Kyra and I just wanted to say hi." She smiled and he walked up on her, pulling her closer to him.

"Where y'all heading after this?" he asked.

He should have already known the answer. Over the last few weeks they had spent a lot of time together, well mostly on the phone or over Kyra's. He knew her father was strict, but he just didn't know how deep it really was for Ari.

After talking for a few more minutes Ari walked back over to Kyra and her friend. The guy he was standing with grabbed her and asked for her number. He was real aggressive and she didn't like that. She was pissed that he'd just snatched her up like that anyway. He was out of line and Ari snatched away hard and gave him the meanest look she could muster up.

"I'm okay, I don't give out my number" She said in a nicer tone. Sure, it could have been easily mistaken for condescending from the look she had given him prior, but it was the truth though. She felt it would be wrong to give a guy her number when Tee was the one who bought the phone for her.

"Bitch fuck you then! You don't gotta give me yo number stuck up hoe! Man, Devin hurry up and get these young bitches away from us dog" he said pushing Ari back.

"Hold on mutha-fucka don't be talking to my friend like dat!" Kyra said jumping in his face. She was way more aggressive than Ari, had a bad temper and stayed ready to put them paws to somebody. She had older brothers and sisters so she wasn't scared to fight. Male or female, if Kyra wanted to fight you she would fight you.

"Kyra it's okay let's just leave" Ari urged pulling her away.

He was drunk and it wasn't any telling what he would do. He seemed like he was too old to be at this party anyway, but it was normal for older people to crash parties around here, like this nigga with a full beard and everything. Ari continued to pull Kyra trying to defuse the situation before it got out of hand. Ari knew that she herself couldn't beat a man and never would try. She didn't want him to hurt Kyra because of her.

"Yeah bitch you better listen to this hoe" the aggressive guy warned coming close up on the two girls again, but this time he mushed Ari in the face, causing her to stumble.

Ari was pissed and all she could do was catch her balance so she wouldn't plummet to the ground and tear up. She grabbed Kyra who was now fighting to get Ari's arms off her so she could get after him, screaming and cussing. Ari looked to his friend for some type of help but the only thing she saw was him getting punched in the face.

"Nigga is you crazy? Don't you ever disrespect her again!" Tommy yelled punching him again.

"Tommy man I'm sorry I didn't know she was wit you!" he said throwing up his hands as if he was anticipating another punch. He had already been knocked on his ass and the guy that Kyra was talking to was sleep too.

Neither of the guys saw Tommy coming just like he liked it. He ran up so quick first knocking the friend out, before the guy he wanted to inflict the most pain upon. He had to make sure that he knew that fucking with Ari was a big mistake.

"Well now you know bitch ass nigga ... All y'all bitch ass niggas better know it!" Tommy screamed at the crowd that was now focused on the drama. He pulled Ari, and his boy grabbed Kyra away, they all climbed into his car and he drove them to Kyra's house.

Tommy didn't play any games when it came to Ari or Ta'Meka Anderson, Tommy's first cousin and the daughter of Uncle Tyson who was the third child of the Anderson boys. It was four uncles all together; Tevin the oldest, Thomas, Tyson and lastly, TaMear who was the baby boy of the Anderson Clan. As a unit and "equals", they ran their drug cartel but we all knew the rankings began with the oldest. They respected their older and wiser brother, he was the brains who kept the family going and the reason they had the city on lock. Thomas and Tyson, born only three days apart, were the reason people feared them. It had been rumored that they'd killed more people than any one person could count. They were the most hot-headed of the brothers and most violent. TaMear was the Virgil, the voice of reason. Everyone depended on to calm any situation that arose.

They were a family and took pride in that. If you were a part of T.A.A; The Anderson Association, which sounded better than referring to themselves as a cartel, they devoted themselves to you. In T.A.A. you had your different crews or camps, as they liked to call them. Each camp worked a different narcotic. There was a camp for weed, a camp for crack cocaine, a heroin camp and a camp that handled pills and lean. Each camp had their own general who ran their particular set. T.A.A. ran the city and surrounding suburbs. They were considered kings where they were from and everyone loved them. They gave back to the families that they were mostly the reasons for them falling apart. Their numbers grew over time, to thirty members or more. Ari had heard a lot of talk that Tommy was the reason for that, but she liked to keep a close ear and a closed mouth when their businesses came into play. She was trained to do so really. Even though Ari wasn't in an intimate relationship with Tommy she was a part of the family, which sometimes caused problems in her current relationships. She couldn't keep away from the family even if she wanted to.

One thing Ari had learned over the years was that loyalty was everything with the Andersons and their Affiliates. Tommy's camp, which included Ari, Kyra, Danny, Meka, Mills, Mia, Chris, Juicy and Justin would take trips and spend time together to solidify their loyalty to their friendship and the association.

----> More Than a Friend <----

"Story of my life, searching for the right, but it keeps avoiding me, sorrow in my soul, because it seems that wrong, really loves my company"

-Rihanna

Chapter 3

Thanks to the boys who had wanted to treat the ladies for the weekend, they were all at a Jamaican Resort in Montego Bay. They claimed the ladies had been distant with each other and made it their priority to bring everyone back together again.

"Omg Tee!" Ari screamed as he came directly after her with his water gun. She was in the middle of posting a picture to her IG that they'd taken the night before at dinner, and he waited until she had gotten dry to taunt her. She smiled hard, thinking about how she loved times like this.

"Bring yo ass back here girl" he shouted as he chased her, feet slightly burning from being on the hot concrete outside of the pool for too long.

"Please stop my phone is ringing!" she screeched, balling up with him standing over her just as he was about to catapult her with water. She pulled her phone from her Pink swimsuit top and answered, "Hello?"

"What are you doing?" Malik asked hearing the girls screaming in the background and Ari laughing.

Malik is Ari's boyfriend and had been for a year now. He was tall, dark and handsome and a wide receiver for the semi-pro Gladiators football team. She could sense the irritation in his voice over the phone. Of course, Ari knew he wasn't pleased with her going on this trip, but he wasn't going to voice it or tell her she couldn't go. Ari felt that she was in control of their relationship and he would never come close to saying anything about her relationship with Tee, or any of the others. He couldn't because she had given Malik the same pep talk that she'd given to the couple other guys who had approached her over the years. Most of them took off for the hills, but she didn't care. If he wasn't man enough to deal with the fact that she was a part of something so powerful, then she didn't need him. He either was in it for the wrong reason or he wasn't tough enough to handle everything she came with. Either way, she was glad they'd got gone.

"You better hurry up because my hands are slipping" Tommy exuberantly towered over her.

Tommy was caramel complexioned. Not really tall, he stood at about 5'11", an average mans' height and towered over her 5'2" petite frame. He now sported a low fade, that gave him a sexy attractiveness after recently cutting off his dreads. They had blond tips that used to sit right above his shoulders, luckily this new look wasn't hard to get used to. He had no bumps, dark spots or craters, nor one mark on his beautiful face. His lips were full and his body was nice. He worked out a lot and it showed. Ari loved his tattoos. She glanced at her name that was stretched across his chest. It was ambigram that read, 'Only Love/Ari'Yonnah'. Rocking with each other for years it wasn't a surprise when he'd gotten it. It was his promise to her that even if they ever decided to separate he'd still be down for her until the end.

"Ahhh baby I'ma call you when I get to the room, they are getting us!" she shrieked.

That's the last thing she was able to say before Tommy sprayed her with water. She laughed and was pissed at the same time. She knew Malik hated her hanging with Tommy, but there wasn't anything that she could do about it because Tommy was going be there no matter what. Even though she loved Malik and thought he was a good guy, Tommy was forever in her eyes. She jumped on Tommy and pushed him into the water. She tossed her phone back onto the poolside chair and jumped in after him. The pool area at the resort was huge and overlooked the ocean. The infinity pool looked as if you were going to swim right into the Caribbean. Ari pulled Tee under and they gazed into each other's eyes. He pointed wanting her to look back so she could see a school of pretty rainbow fish on the other side. She turned and touched the thick glass that separated them from the ocean. Her chest tightened and when she came up for air she saw the others.

"Kyra, Meka, Ari, Mia help me!" Juicy screamed as Justin dunked her.

"Meka, behind you!" Mia screamed just as Chris grabbed her pushing her in the pool, and Mills in turn grabbed Meka.

Kyra bust out laughing and Tommy pulled her in with Danny's help. Ari laughed. She loved her family, they were all she had. Through thick and thin they had each other's back regardless of what it entailed. They protected each other and didn't let too many outsiders in their circle. They were loyal to each other, which was a T.A.A. unwritten rule. They all left the pool area and headed to the suites.

Ari's room and Tee's room were connected, in one luxurious suite. They were the only one's there who were not with their significant other's so they stuck together. It was expected anyway, Tee made sure to keep her close at all times. Ari knew that he messed around other girls, but he never admitted to being in an actual relationship. He always claimed he was getting money out here and that's all that mattered. She didn't care if he messed with girls or if he did decide to get into another relationship. She just wanted whoever he chose to be his woman to be top notch like the rest of the ladies and nothing less. She had to be a rider, period.

Ari didn't waste any time showering as she waited for the next excursion to take place. All she really wanted to do have dinner and go to bed. She couldn't wait to catch the flight back home the next day. She wasn't used to being away from Malik this long ever since they'd been together. She normally spent weekends and nights with him, which was another reason she was with the family now. The family felt as though she had been keeping to herself more lately, trying to blame Malik for that. She was still the same Ari, inside and out. She was getting to the point where she didn't find the need to be with them day in and day out. Everyone was grown and what was acceptable when they were younger wasn't acceptable now. She was starting to become overwhelmed with trying to balance Malik and Tommy. If she was with one the other felt neglected, and vice versa. She needed and wanted 'Ari' time so badly.

*****

"I don't wanna do this anymore, I don't wanna be the reason why, every time I walk out the door, I see him die a little more inside, I don't wanna hurt him anymore I don't wanna take away his life"

-Rihanna

Ari entered the condo that she shared with Malik. It was nicely decorated and dimly lit. When you walked into the first room you could see a big white sectional. Placed on the sectional were six different gold, lavender and white accent pillows, which complemented the white and gold color scheme in the room. She didn't usually let visitors sit in the living room so there wasn't a T.V. or anything remotely entertaining. The white walls had a few pictures spread across for decoration, but not a single picture of Malik and her together on the walls. She hadn't noticed that until now. She didn't know why she hadn't put any up; it wasn't like they didn't have any together, she thought to herself as she wandered down the hallway. First searching in the bedroom, bathrooms, and kitchen she then checked the basement where she found Malik peacefully sleeping.

"Hey baby," she greeted kissing him.

"Hey, baby how you doing?" he rose up, pulling her onto his lap.

"Was missing you, but I'm good now, how are you?" she replied kissing him again.

"Good" he managed to say through kisses.

Ari hated leaving him and often felt like maybe she should focus on them more and leave her other life behind. Well not necessarily behind, but take time to focus more on her and Malik, and building their foundation. They had come to a place in their relationship where things weren't too good. Malik never wanted her to go out and he was always thinking something was up with her. Mama, Tee's mom, would always tell her "a man who finds himself always accusing you of something is either insecure or is doing something he had no business doing." She would look Ari in the eyes and tell her, "Child it's up to you to decide which it is. A man makes time for who and what is important to him." Ari later realized that was Mama's way of telling her that Tee was doing dirt on her, but that was her baby and she wasn't going hate on him. She laughed a little and never let that make her feel any type of way. Ari respected Tommy's family because loyalty and trust was what they stood for, so how could she expect anything less. They were like family to her; so, when it came out later in Ari and Tommy's relationship that Tommy was messing around on her, and couldn't for the life of him be faithful, they held her down just like they would if it had been Meka.

Ari shook the thought out her head, she could never imagine life without Kyra, Tee, and Meka, she couldn't imagine living without them. They were all she really had and if they weren't around she didn't know what she would do. She needed them and believed they needed her just as much. They had been click tight for so many years now, shutting everyone else out. She had no family; Kyra had basically disowned hers after her mother too had passed away, so they were all each other had and Ari was okay with that.

Ari straddled Malik while his hands roamed her body. Slipping his shirt off, he slipped off hers and took her left breast into his mouth. She moaned as she felt the warmth of his breath blow against her nipple, causing it to harden instantly. He took his time suckling, flicking his tongue up and down, which drove Ari crazy. She'd never realized how much she enjoyed having her tits sucked until Malik. He had taught her a few things over the past few months. His lips traveled from the hard nipple to her mouth debauchedly kissing her. Not wanting any foreplay and not really a "kisser", Ari unzipped his pants and slipped his hard member into her already wet "Kitty Boo".

Moaning in pleasure, she grinded her hips and bounced up and down as they continued to kiss. Trying not to lose focus, absolutely hating to do this much kissing, she continued knowing Malik liked to kiss. She was on top and in control, enjoying the ride so she dealt with it. She tightened her walls each time she rose and dropped down, gripping his manhood. It took everything in her not to swing her arms like a cowgirl taming her beast, like a bull rider attempting to stay mounted while the animal attempted to buck her off. Ari forcefully moved her face away from his and allowed him to suck on her neck, not able to take his wet kisses anymore. He gripped her neck and sucked hard while holding on to her body still thrusting up in her love canal hard. She fought to get up but he tightened his grip, making sure she felt everything he had built up in him. Before she knew it, she had released her juices all over his dick.

"You like that shit, don't you?" Malik grunted pulling her long jet black hair so hard her neck snapped back. He pumped a few more strokes before he also reached his climax. He softened up, kissing her neck and chest gentler than before.

"I love you Ari," he confessed looking into her pretty honey eyes.

"I love you too boo!" she gave him one last kiss before hopping off his lap, letting everything he'd released inside her pour back out onto him.

After the quickie, Ari rushed into the shower to change clothes. She sashayed into the room dressed in a cute black Vera Wang dress, a black pair of Louboutin's with a silver spiked heel, and sprayed a little Marc Jacobs "Daisy" on to complement her beauty. She not only looked good she smelled divine. Ari sported a pair of 1 ½ carat white gold diamond earrings and a 3-carat choker necklace, courtesy of Tommy. He always purchased gifts for her out of the blue and told her if he got one she would too. When Tommy purchased something for himself he always checked to see if it came in Ari's size. She knew there would come a day when she would have to turn down his gifts, but fortunately for her that day hadn't come around yet.

"Where you going?" Malik questioned. Ari could tell from his instant attitude he already knew the answer. She also knew that they were going to have it out because of it.

"Tonight's the night we're having dinner with the uncles, you know that," Ari answered irritated and not up for any confrontation. Their fuck session had her feeling good and she wanted to hold on to that.

Once a month the Anderson family had dinner with the uncles and two times a month T.A.A had "meetings" to attend. The dinner was specifically to bring together the family. Each uncle brought their families and only close friends attended. Mostly the friends of the uncles who grew up with them and were no longer in the game.

At the meetings, the people who attended were Tommy's father and uncles, the top generals in each distribution operation or camps, their wives, wifeys or longterm girlfriends. Over the many years, they'd have these meetings, none of the participating ladies knew who dealt what or anything close to it other than the camp they were in. They knew of each other but didn't really communicate amongst themselves, only the main generals in their respective sets did. From Tommy's camp, only Ari and Meka were allowed to attend, and the only men were Mills and Tommy. Kyra, Danny, Juicy, Justin, Mia and Chris were all very important to T.A.A, but hadn't gained the trust from the uncles yet to attend. Ari assumed that's just how things worked. She had mixed feelings about the meetings and didn't see why anyone in their right minds would want to attend. She also knew that T.A.A was doing the right thing with having them.

"You just got home." Malik's irritation spread across his face and hers too.

"I promise I won't stay for drinks tonight, I'll come straight back." She compromised knowing he hated her going to these dinners and meetings. He didn't even know the half of what they entailed. The dinners were a way for them to bond as a family, and being the type of family the Anderson's and affiliates are they needed time to do that.

The meetings, on the other hand, were different. She would much rather miss a meeting than a dinner. The dinners were always catered by Uncle Tevin's personal chief. It almost seemed like a movie with the ladies coming out dressed in their maid attire, standing around in uniform to serve dinner in style. The table in the dining area was big and cherry wood. It seated about twenty or more people and all the chairs were filled. They were comfortable and each person had a designated seat. Their sitting arrangements were by couple and family. Tommy, his mama, pops, and Ari all sat together. The food was always magnificent and she always had a glass of champagne or wine to go with her meal since she wasn't a drinker. Uncle Tevin always spoke during the dinners. Ari loved her family and was blessed to be a part of something so great.

"I don't understand why you need to be at these dinners or better yet, why your man can't attend them with you."

"Because Tommy wants me by his side, and that's where I am going to be! Besides, we a family baby and you know good and well you ain't try'na sit around me and the family." she side- eyed him knowing he was full of shit. He always froze up whenever anyone from camp came around him.

"You act like you fucking him."

"OMG here we go again" she sighed.

"Yeah here we go again, are you fucking him?" he asked now in her face.

Sometimes she wished he was from the hood so he could understand how real it was out there and the weight the Anderson family carried. She knew that he knew about them, but to him it was unrealistic for one family to have so much power. She tried to explain that it was no different from any rich white family, they were just hood. They carried just as much weight in the streets and judicial system as white rich folks.

"First, you need to back the fuck up and secondly, you know I'm not fucking him" Ari said backing away because he didn't budge.

"I don't know! That's why I asked" he spat, still in her face.

"I don't have time for this."

Hearing her phone ring Ari knew Tommy was at the door. She turned and hurried out, knowing this argument could go on for hours if she'd let it. Tommy had already gotten out of the black Tahoe to open the door for her. Ari climbed in, securing her seat belt as Tommy slid into the driver's seat. Admiring the inside of his truck she could tell he had recently upgraded it and it was dope. He'd had it customized so everything was touch screen and voice activated, set to both of their voices. She didn't have to assume because everything he did he made sure she had all access to it.

It had gotten dark outside and the night air was cool. Ari resided on a very quiet street so it seemed as if it was only them. No cars were parked in the front of any houses or other condos, just her and Tommy. She looked out the window back towards her condo and saw Malik looking out the window. It hurt her deeply to know that she was hurting him, but at this point she had no idea what to do. These were the times she wished she had a mama to call and confide in, but she didn't. Ari wished she could lay on her mother's bed with her head gently resting on her mother's thighs and cry her eyes out about everything going on in her life or what Ari felt was missing. She suspected that if her mother was alive she would probably not be in this situation. There would be no Tee and family. Ari knew her mom was the missing part of her life. Losing her mother so early in life left a void. Ari still remembered it like yesterday; the moment her life changed, the day she started to *exist*.

Ari walked off the stage and took a seat with the rest of her team. It was their City-Wide Talent Showcase and her team, who was named Synergy, had been the best for what seemed like forever for the young girls, and now another competing team was trying to take their title. She was captain along with Kyra, the one who came up with most of the team's distinct and unique dance moves. Their moves were so tight and legit they made people forget about the stanky leg, creep, and bounce. People all over Philly were doing Synergy's moves. Yeah, Synergy was popular for their moves around where they stayed. Ari could do a lot of things, but dancing was what she felt she was greatest in.

As the last team took the stage, Synergy noticed the first part of the competing team's routine were moves from Synergy's performance last year. The whole crowd noticed and started to boo. Synergy had a saying for females who jacked their style, so they all jumped up screaming "Blueprint! BlllllluuuuuueeeeeePprrrinnnttt" to let them know they had indeed noticed that they'd stolen their style. Ari was so happy when they told her that her team won first place again. She was only ten so this meant a lot to her. She looked in the audience for her mom and neither her mother nor her father was there. She caught a ride home with Kyra's mom and when they arrived there were several cops at their house. Kyra and her mom walked with Ari into the house.

"Hey dad, what's wrong? Where's mom?" She asked looking at his tear stained face.

"Baby there is something I have to tell you," his voice bleated.

"No I don't care! Where is mom?!" She cried fearing what he would tell her next.

"She's gone baby, your mom is gone" he lamented for his wife, grabbing his daughter into one of the tightest hugs he had ever given her.

"Nooooo daddy you're lying! Where is my mom?!" she wailed her honey-eyes filled with tears of sorrow.

Ari looked at Kyra who was now crying and being consoled by her mom. She left her daddy's arms and her and Kyra hugged and cried together.

Ari was drained when everyone left, emotionally and physically. Her dad sat downstairs drinking everything in his liquor cabinet. It was late when he came into her room.

"You bitch it's all your fault!" he screamed throwing the empty Vodka bottle at her. It crashed into the wall and glass flew all over her bed. She jumped and warm piss cascaded down her leg soaking her pink Tuesday panties. She pulled the glass covered blanket up under her neck, staring at his red eyes as he glared at her. He was so angry and Ari didn't know why. It wasn't like she was ever a daddy's girl. Ari and her mother were always closer than her father and she were. She never cared because her mom gave her all the love she needed.

"Daddy!" she screamed crying, voice trembling. she was petrified. She had never seen her daddy drink or get this angry before. He was so loving when it came to her mother.

"She died trying to make it to your stupid competition" he said pulling her out the bed by her hair.

Ari's father threw her to the floor and kicked her repeatedly. She cried, begging him to stop. He screamed how much he hated her and how she should have never been born. He beat her so bad she couldn't go to school *for a week. She had lost her mother and her father in one night.*

"Everything good?" Tee asked knowing instantly something was wrong. Ari hated when he did that. He could sometimes look at her and tell her exactly what she was thinking. That's the type of connection they had. He always read her like a book.

"Of course," she said smiling as he grabbed her hand and turned up the music. She heard Young Glizzy's voice fill the truck. Tommy and Ari rode in silence as she bobbed her head to "Lil Mama" and she knew he'd chosen that song because she was indeed his li'l mama. She wasn't going anywhere any time soon if she had anything to do with it. She would continue to ride with Tee, for as long as he wanted her to.

----> More Than a Friend <----

"Things have gotten difficult, try to be Mr. Perfect intercontinental, hold up you spend your time with your friends all the time and all that time with your friends put my momentum on decline"

-Wale

Chapter 4

Ari entered the dark condo, exhausted from the monthly meeting with the family, and was happy to see Malik sleeping. Little did he know he was her serenity after the arduous meetings she was required to attend. Even though she leveled up years ago, the physical stresses were now mental. She slipped out of her black Nike jogging suit, and showered she was always tired after the meetings; they always mentally and physically drained her. She laid next to him, watching him sleep for a minute. Ari loved him, but that didn't stop the thoughts she sometimes had when she considered being single. Taking Malik's arms Ari wrapped them around her waist, snuggling under his warm body. She was surprised and a little hurt when he moved them and hastily flipped over.

"Why you do that?" she asked, glancing over her shoulder at him. She'd had a long night and all she wanted was him to wrap his big arms around her and make her feel better. She wasn't in the mood to argue, she could barely keep her eyes open as it was.

"Just go to sleep" he mumbled, continuing to lay with his eyes closed and back towards her.

Malik was tired and didn't know how much longer he could take this. He loved Ari with his all, but he was tired of her dinners, late meetings and vacations. Ari never included him in anything that she did with her so called quote, un quote family, but wanted him to just sit around and wait on her. She came home with expensive gifts, flaunting everything that they did for her in his face. He was done. He felt as though they were no longer in love like she claimed they were they merely co*existed*. They weren't living life like he had dreamed when he decided to make her his girl and moved her into his 200,000-dollar condo. He dreamed of them being happy together just the two of them. He didn't have a family and neither did Ari and that was one thing that he loved about her. She was supposed to be his and only his.

"No, we go through this every week. You know I'ma be there for Tommy no matter what! Like what part of that don't you understand? I told you when we first got together that I was best friends with him and that he was going to be here!"

Everything Ari said was the truth. That's why she'd made it a priority to tell whoever she dated what it is from the beginning. Tommy was her best friend and she knew the type of relationship they shared was normally hard to deal with. Ari couldn't understand herself, what man would actually be okay with Tee and her? She'd always ride with Tee, Kyra and Meka, and if a man couldn't handle that he could keep it moving. Malik had chosen to stay, she wasn't sure why, but it was something she hated to ponder on. She was too tired and frustrated to debate this with him tonight, just like she was last week before the dinner.

"Do that mean you have to take trips, go to dinners, and wear all the diamonds and shit he buys you?" he asked hastily flipping over again to face her.

She knew then he was insecure and jealous of Tee, which was a personal problem that he would have to solve on his own. Tee and Ari hadn't slept together since she was 17-years old, and he didn't even know that. She felt Malik needed to let this go.

"Is that the problem?" She said leaping out the bed. "You mad because he buys me things? Things you can't afford to buy me?" she regretted the words as soon as they left her mouth.

He jumped up from the bed and grabbed Ari, slamming her on the ground. Shocked was to say the least because he'd never touched her throughout their entire relationship. He was always so gentle with her and never showed her any sign that he would actually do something physical. She froze for a second, positive he could see the fear written on her face. Suddenly, she was 12-years old again.

Ari was sitting in her old bedroom, purple and white wall paper covered the walls with pretty green and purple butterflies printed throughout. Her carpet was lavender and it had two pretty white rugs with green and purple butterflies printed on them. One rug was placed at the entrance to her room and the other was sitting under the chair to her vanity. She had a flat screen Sony T.V mounted on the wall and she was watching 'Bring it on' while combing her hair, until she was overcome with a throbbing pain in her head. Her father was standing over her, after coming into her room and throwing her onto her head screaming, "why are there dishes in my sink?!" He left just as quickly as he had come. He was drunk again and she was dizzy, very dizzy.

Getting up Ari grabbed her brown checkered Louis Vuitton tote-purse and keys. Before he could apologize she was out the door and in the car. She took a deep breath and headed in the direction she was so used to driving in. The night air chilled her thick thighs, sending chill bumps throughout her body. She was upset with herself for not slipping into some sweats or something before storming out. She turned the heat up in the car and heard the soft voice of Maxwell's *'Pretty Wings'*. Letting his smooth voice set the mood the entire drive her thoughts were clouded. She thought about Malik and their relationship, and if it would last. She considered just being single, but she wasn't sure how things would work. She was in a different position with this relationship, her and Malik actually lived together. If they were to break up she would be the one to move, but where would she go? Arriving at her destination Ari pulled into the driveway and knew the answers to her questions.

She had really come to a place in her heart where she felt as if everything around her wasn't what she wanted. She had just finished school and needed a job before she could feel comfortable living alone, but honestly, she was willing to take that leap of faith. She thought every woman eventually comes to a point in her life where she should be alone to work on herself. Ari had come to the point where she was beginning to ruminate whether she was really *living*. She didn't want to be the same person she had been over the years, depending on the people around her to bring her joy. She didn't want to *exist* in the state she was in right now where she lived through other people, creating her personality, thoughts and opinions based on what society thought. Mainly what the family thought. She didn't know how she had come to the point where she didn't know which way was up?

----> More Than a Friend <----

"She still got a nigga back, know that's for sure, no matter what may occur in life, every day with her is like a plus, I'ma love her til' she be like that's enough."

-T.I.

Chapter 5

    Tommy was trying to relax after getting home from the meeting. He had a lot of things to put together and he couldn't move too fast on any of it. Like on most days his thoughts drifted to Ari. He knew it was hard on her, but she was the only one he trusted with any and everything, including his life. Flicking through the channels he heard a knock on his door. Tommy instinctually grabbed his strap and opened it without asking who it was. Everyone knew to call before they came so he was confused as to who could be here so late.

    "Damn Tee it's just me" Ari flinched her heart skipping a beat. She loved that he was always alert, but also hated it because it made her worry about him. Even though Ari was aware that her best friend lived a dangerous lifestyle she never wanted to think about anything happening to him or any other T.A.A member.

    Feeling bad that he upped the strap on her, Tommy stored his 9mm back into his holster that was still clipped to his black polo sweat-suit and checked her out. She was standing in some really short pajama shorts and a cami with no bra. Her nipples were hard, poking straight through the shirt. Tommy's eyes shot down to her camel-toe sitting fat. She was so gorgeous to him and he just stared taking in every inch of her coke bottle shape, thick thighs and flawless yellow skin. Like every time he saw her he was flooded with different emotions. Tommy wanted her badly, but knew she deserved better. When he said better he meant a man that had time for her and could do lame shit, like movies and ice cream on the beach. Tommy wasn't a hearts and flowers type of nigga. He was a street nigga inside and out. Fucking with Ari's ass sometimes made him soft and he had to remind himself that shit wasn't him and get back to the coldhearted, grinder that he really was. He couldn't get soft for no bitch, not even Ari. That's why he didn't push for her to be his bitch. He let her have her li'l boyfriends and shit, but still showered her with diamonds, Louis bags, and Red Bottoms. At the end of the day when it came to the streets and she was out and about, niggas knew she was down with the team and Tommy knew she was going to carry herself as such.

"Well, what you doing here? You have a key anyways, why you knock?" he wondered, stepping aside, letting her in while scoping out the block before shutting the door. Usually she would have used her key so he needed to know why this night was different.

"I just needed to get away" she said taking a seat on the couch, picking up his drink and sipping it. "Ugh what is this?" she frowned putting it back down.

Even her frown was beautiful and it made him chuckle a little. He had put a stop to that shit before she'd even tried to start. No woman that he fucked with was going to be out here drunk and shit, not carrying herself boss-like. Tommy didn't give a fuck about what those other niggas did with their hoes, but his bitch wasn't going to do it. He believed she was now to the point she didn't even want to drink.

"Girl that's a grown man's drink, Henny and Coke" he laughed again because she couldn't even handle a sip of drank and the cute face she made had his manhood rising. "What happened, why you need to get away?" he quizzed making sure he didn't have to go whoop on boy for fucking with her. Tommy had done that plenty of times and he wouldn't hesitate to do it again. He had no problem with coming, fucking shit up and keeping it fucking moving. He had no problems shooting a nigga, but he enjoyed and preferred beating him the fuck up and having that fear control on him forever. When it came to Ari it was another thing, he would kill for her. She'd had a rough start to life so he made sure every day that she was *living* now and living well. He'd made it a point long ago when he first met her ass to make her his. Tommy reminisced about it like it was yesterday when he first locked eyes with her fatty.

These niggas were playing games and Tommy wasn't for it. He needed all his cash in full because he'd already fronted them niggas three balls the day before. At least one nigga from the camp had better run him his money. He'd had to prove to the uncles it was a good idea to start up a camp in the lower eastside. A place that was so grimy even the uncles didn't fuck around. Those team eastside niggas were greasy and didn't care about life. Most of them niggas lived off bitches so their 'get money' game was off. He saw it as a challenge and gave a few of them propositions he knew no real man could refuse, so he knew everything he had was put on the line.

Tommy chilling with his brother QB looked up and noticed this ass across the street. He had seen shorty before, but today was different. She had on some blue jean shorts and a pink beater and a pair of corny ass reeboks. He shook his head, shorty needed to step her game up or a nigga to do it for her. Hey, he felt he might be the man for the job. Tommy rubbed his hands together like he was about to feast on a meal.

"Check out shorty ass!" QB said as if he didn't already see him watching it.

"Nigga I been peeped game!" Tommy said not being able to tear his eyes away even if he'd tried.

"Nigga shorty young as a bitch, I think she wit' Kaison's li'l sister" Danny chimed in, "I went to school with her brother."

"Her shoe game whack, yeah she gotta be young," QB said and turned around to finish freaking his mild.

"Shit I a fuck on li'l bitch and buy her some shoes for a li'l while," Tommy stated and yelled across the street.

"*Aye, cutie what's yo name?*" he screamed checking to see if she was thirsty and going to run over to him. He always tested a bitch by the way he pulled up on them. If she came to him he knew he had her. If he had to go to her he knew she may be worth the chase. Tommy was a boss and everybody knew it so he never had to chase for too long, IF he had to at all. Shorty looked back and turned around again.

"*Aye ma I'm talking to you!*" he pointed making sure she knew he was talking to her. She stopped but didn't say anything, just looked at him. "*Come here,*" he waved her over to him. She stood there not saying anything. Is this hoe retarded? He thought to himself and started walking across the street. As he approached her and her friend, he noticed she was light skinned with long jet black hair that looked real, and she had natural honey colored eyes.

"*Damn ma you beautiful*" he complimented.

"*Whatever*" she replied smiling and he could tell she was shy.

He liked shy girls. Tommy had fucked a couple shy girls that weren't so shy when they had a dick in them. Their true selves came out when a nigga was gutting them deep.

"*I'm Tommy, what's yo name?*" he asked licking his lips. He knew that was one of his good features, Tommy felt all girls looked at a niggas lips first, most thinking *about riding a nigga's face, but he didn't get down like that though. Wasn't no hoe going to be pumping her pussy on his face like he was lame nigga. He was gulley, he fucked faces. Tommy knew how they thought though, so he kept his full lips up to par, moisturized not glossy.*

"I'm Ari, this is Kyra" she said introducing herself and her friend.

He could tell by the way her voice trembled that she was nervous. He couldn't help but to hope and pray shorty wasn't a virgin or something. He didn't need any problems. Tommy hated popping hoes cherries and then they thought you're supposed to lock them down or something. She was cute though and he could tell for sure she was innocent. Hmmm innocent Ari, it had a ring to it. Tommy looked up to see Mark's red 07' Monte Carlo driving slowly up the street. He had to hurry and get li'l ma's number because he didn't want her to see him smack one of these niggas if they didn't have his money.

"Well I gotta go but I wanna get yo number," he said taking out his cellphone.

"Sorry Tommy but I'm not allowed to have boys call" she responded sheepishly.

"Even yo cell phone?" he asked not believing her and wondering how young she was.

"I don't have one" she said focusing on the ground.

Tommy could tell she was embarrassed. Maybe her family was church going or something and didn't believe in that. "Well look do this, I'ma be here tomorrow so come back here at like twelve because I don't wanna go too long without hearing yo voice or seeing yo pretty face."

She smiled again before saying she would. He jogged across the street and already had it planned. He was going to buy her a burner phone and give it to her tomorrow. But first to this money.

"Tee, he just makes me mad sometimes" Ari whined lying on his legs.

"Well you welcome to stay here. You want me to get the guestroom ready?" he asked her because she was already dozing off.

"Ummmhmmm" she mumbled, never opening her eyes.

He scooped her up and carried her to the back, steadily admiring her pretty, long black hair and her yellow eyelids and long natural eye lashes that covered her honey brown eyes. She had the smoothest, unflawed yellow skin. What he liked to call the total package.

She was real shy, even still with Tommy after all the years, and everything they'd been through. She also had a temper when she wanted to have one. He'd never been on that side of her anger. Out of all her friends, including his loud and ghetto cousin, Meka, Ari was the quiet one and that's why he'd always admired her. That's why he had always been fond of Ari and looked out for her since he was a few years older. Tommy knew way more about life and way more about *living* than she did. He was humble; he understood that you had to treasure life, everything, and everyone, in it. He had always looked out for Ari and made sure no one ever fucked with her, including her family. She was a good girl and that's why he tried to keep her out of his dangerous life style.

She had just finished hair school at 21-years old and managed to obtain a manager's license also, since she wanted to own her own shop one day. Who knew, he might buy one for her. He was willing to invest because he knew she was worth it, every penny.

Tommy laid her in his bed and slipped into the black 1,000 count spread next to her after checking the house one more time. Looking down at her he considered going into the guest room, but said fuck it and propped up on his elbow. He enjoyed the site as she slept below him. Tommy could not stop thinking about how good that shit felt to sleep next to a woman who fucked with you out of love, and not for money. One of his main reasons why he didn't show any of these hoes any attention right now. He felt it was li'l nigga shit. He was past trying to fuck every girl in the world. He was trying to fuck one bad bitch while he gained enough trust from his uncles and pops to run their empire. They were getting old and you'd think he would've been promoted since he'd doubled their size. QB and Tommy were both with the shit, they were made for it. Running the Association would be little to nothing long as he had his nigga by his side and he knew that's where QB was going to be. Tommy spent most of his days trying to get shit together and yeah it was hard for him, but you had to do what you had to do. He would never want to step on his family's toes but honestly, he was over this general shit, he was trying to be big dog.

----> More Than a Friend <----

"You think I'd leave your side baby? You know me better than that You think I'd leave you down when your down on your knees? I wouldn't do that, I'll do you right when your wrong if only you could see into me"

-Sade

<u>Chapter 6</u>

Ari woke up early to Tommy sitting on the edge of the bed watching T.V. and talking on the phone.

"Morning" he greeted her never once attempting to turn around, she always wondered how he did that. Stretching Ari sat up; after being worn out from the meeting last night and the spat she'd had with Malik a good night's rest was needed. She looked around and took everything in, from his white carpet and black painted walls, down to his black and white plush comforter she had tightly wrapped around her coke bottle frame. She was short, but definitely had a nice body something she got from her mama.

Her mother was a dime and Ari could remember her beautiful features like she'd seen her yesterday. She was also short, standing at about 5'2" and she too had an ass on her. Ari's mother had a caramel complexion and pretty brown eyes. Always wearing her hair short, it was thick and black like Ari's. Her mother loved to do hair and often changed up her styles. Ari's heart became heavy thinking about her mother and she knew that she couldn't let that bring her down. Thinking about her mother has sent her into depression several times and she had enough going on in her life right now to let that happen. She wished she could think about the happy times she and her mother shared, without that happening but unfortunately that never happened and she'd often land in a place she didn't want to be.

Looking up at Tommy's 65" 4k Ultra T.V. mounted on the wall she noticed he was watching the news. That was one of the things she did love about him. He was very smart and intelligent, always keeping up with what was going on in the world. He watched all the news channels, everything from CNN down to the local news stations. He was into politics and very multicultural. He was socially capable of being placed in any environment and he would adapt. Another reason he was favored by the uncles.

"How you know I was awake?" she yawned still feeling drowsy. He shrugged his shoulders and continued his conversation.

Ari sauntered into the connecting bathroom and grabbed an extra tooth brush. She was familiar with his place because her and Meka decorated for him. His bathroom was small but perfect for one person. Like the bedroom, the bathroom's walls also had a deep tone that created a cozy and homely environment, black and gold marble countertop, an under-mounted sink, with black raised panel cabinets. It housed a Jacuzzi tub, an open shower, and a one-piece toilet. Her bare feet glided comfortably across the black and gray stone travertine tiled floors. As she brushed her teeth and gazed into the mirror she contemplated what would happen when she returned home. Trying to focus on the positives, she couldn't stop thinking about the many things in her life that were changing and her perpetual feeling of uneasiness with the decisions she had been making recently.

Back into Tommy's room, checking her phone she had voicemails from Malik. She figured he was probably apologizing for what he did and she had every intention on forgiving him.

"You have three new voice messages, click one to ... message one, hey baby this Malik," he paused then the recording continued, "I'm sorry for what I did, can you please come home so we can talk about this? Ari, you mean everything to me baby and I just want you here. Anyway, I love you! Please come home." The recorder came back on, "End of message one, to keep press ... you have kept message one. Message two ..." the phone beeped and message two started. "What up sis you know who this is, call me Love. You know the ladies going out to dinner tonight, can you come get me?" The message ended.

Making a mental note to call Kyra back, Ari decided to just hang up and not listen to the rest of the messages. It wasn't any doubt, she was going to forgive Malik. After changing clothes, Tommy had finally completed his call and now was watching T.V. periodically glancing at Ari as she moved gracefully across the room.

"That's a shame your bed so damn big your feet dangle" she laughed, cracking up at her own joke.

"Hahaha, you so damn funny" he pretended to laugh. "What you doing today?" he questioned candidly.

"I have to go to a few shops and see who got a station open and then I don't know. I think me and the ladies having dinner tonight." Ari shrugged her classic formed shoulders and stared down at him with her honey brown eyes that he loved so much. She couldn't help but to stare at him also, loving his baby face. His rectangular shaped head and chiseled chin made him very appealing, and easy on the eyes.

At first glance you would not be able to tell baby was a thug. He looked like he could model or work at a bank or something. It was when you got to the thousand dollar chains, watches, and shoes that exposed him for what he really was. The way he strutted in a clean pair of Jay's and all black Polo sweats you could tell he was a gangster.

"Ai'ight well hit me up later or something" he responded and pushed himself all the way back to the black, leather, Onyx ornament embellished, headboard. The king-sized bed was made for royalty and had a traditional theme with a modern twist. She agreed and giggled, exiting as she thought to herself, "his li'l ass."

After stopping by a few shops, she couldn't prolong her return home. Ari had no idea how the conversation would take place between the two once he got home from practice. She was happy to know she had a little more time to gather her thoughts. She wanted to be with this man and love him like he deserved, but lately a relationship just hadn't been what she was feeling, her actions reflecting that. She knew that was her problem, and she didn't know what she wanted. Ari sighed and sauntered up to the condo door. She was surprised to see Malik sitting there, chilling in his full practice gear she had expected him to be gone.

"You ain't having practice?" she asked taking a seat next to him.

"Naw, where were you last night? Baby I'm so sorry for what I did."

Malik really did feel some kind of way about slamming Ari. He loved her and hadn't slept all night worried about how she was feeling. She rushed out of there so fast, she didn't give him enough time to even make sure if she was okay. He was worried about her being hurt and worried that she would run to her quote, unquote best friend. The last thing he needed right now was to be dealing with her fake thug ass best friend and their so-called dangerous family. He was stressed out enough being released from the team. Little did Ari know he was worried that she would leave him because he couldn't provide her with the things that Tommy could. He had been working so hard trying to make it to the NFL, so he could follow his dreams and do something that she could be proud of him for doing, but that all changed with one phone call from the team's manager notifying him of his release from the team. His personal manager had called him last night and told him they were considering letting him go and she wasn't there. She was too busy being there for Tommy. She wasn't there when he needed her to be.

"I know and it's okay" she said letting him know that she wasn't tripping off it. She could tell by the look in his eyes that he meant what he had said. She also knew she was dead wrong for emasculating him like she had when she said what she said. Ari knew he was struggling, trying to get drafted and that he did buy her nice things when he was able to. She decided that she had to do better when it came to him. He was different from the few men she had dealt with in the past she had never dealt with a sensitive man before. Like always her thoughts drifted to Tee, he was far from sensitive, or at least she felt. Malik and Ari chilled together until about 7:00 that evening before she prepared herself for an interesting girls night with the ladies. They often had dinner with each other once a month as a way to keep in touch and keep each other posted on things going on in their lives. Every girl in their camp had at least one girl that they talked to on a daily, Meka and Kyra were hers.

----> More Than a Friend <----

"True friendships are everlasting, daily conversations aren't needed, they don't care about the outside, it's all about what's in your heart"

Chapter 7

All the girls were chilling and laughing. They all loved their ladies' nights because it gave them a chance to catch up and really make each other feel better. Of course, Juicy was being Juicy telling everyone about her rendezvous with Ty'Shon last night. Juicy's name fits her well; she was thick as hell but a pretty thick chick, and she was put together tight. Plus-sized but not sloppy. She was also that ghetto, uneducated, ratchet, every stereotype of a drug dealer's girlfriend and she wore it well. Dropping out of school when they were all in the 8th grade she was loud and obnoxious. You would never think she was as big as she was because she thought she was the "baddest" thing walking, demanding attention from everyone in the room. You couldn't tell her shit and that's what Ari loved about her. She was loyal and would do anything for any of the girls. Now when it came to her relationship Ari couldn't speak on it. Juicy had it bad for a long dick and a fat blunt.

"Giiiirrrrlllllaaaaaa when I say he did everything right he did EVERYTHING right," laughing loud as hell like always Juicy grinded her hips like she was riding an imaginary dick and had the nerve to lick her fingers and pat her vagina.

"Well on another note Malik slammed me yesterday" Ari confided and everybody paused and their eyes darted in her direction. The mood of the conversation changed from their laughing about Juicy's wild sex life to shoot em' up murder, murder.

"Run that back" Meka snapped her neck in Ari's direction mad as hell. You could see it all on her face. Her dark brown eyes pierced through Ari as if she was staring her down like they were in an old western movie about to have a duel. Glaring at her like she was reading her mind trying to get a hint or any connotative meaning out of what Ari was about to say.

"Well he was upset and I didn't make it better and he just kind of picked me up and threw me down," Ari continued almost like it was nothing, taking another sip of her virgin daiquiri. She honestly felt that way, and it's not like he had done that before. Malik had never treated her with anything other than respect throughout the year they'd been together. He's always treated her like how she thought a woman should be treated. He catered to her in a sense. He supported her financially; never asking her to pay any bills, she didn't have to work, was able to finish school and he was loyal to her. He didn't know about the monthly stipend she received from Uncle Tevin so he thought he was doing it all. On another note, she'd never been approached by a woman claiming they were sleeping with him, despite his occupation. She looked at Meka and knew she was definitely going to tell Tommy.

"And don't tell Tee Meka" Ari looked at her reading her thoughts. They knew each other so well. Meka was like her big sister, her backbone. They talked to each other about everything and even though Meka was older than her, Ari was her walking diary. The day that Tommy first introduced them she had Ari's back, just like the rest of his family.

"What's up?" This girl about Ari's height and her skin complexion asked her as she rested in the front seat of Tommy's car, waiting for him to come back out his Uncle's house. The girl had on a pair of black jeans and a red and black Hollister hoodie. She rocked a pair of red and black varsity Air Retro Jordan 11's. Ari recognized them because Tommy had bought her the same pair. Ari was starting to keep up on the "fads" or up-to- date kicks and trends that were always coming out because of Tommy. If he had them she had them. He looked out for her.

"Hi," Ari replied shyly. She had never met this girl and didn't know why he'd left them outside together. Ari was definitely nervous and now wished that Kyra had come with them on this "ride" he wanted her to take with him.

"I'm Ta'Meka," she introduced herself and continued, "but everybody calls me Meka."

"Hi, I'm Ari."

"I know, you think I don't know who in my cousin's car?" She rolled her dark brown eyes at Ari and moved her neck in one swift snake-like motion. Her long fingernails were blue and were covered with a lot of different designs.

"Well even if you did I was letting you know out of courtesy," Ari responded not really meaning to sound as mean as she had come off. She was getting hot and irritated because Tommy was taking forever to come out the house.

"Well excuse me," Meka said and turned to walk away.

Just then two girls from Ari's school were walking past and spotted her in Tommy's car. They always thought it was funny to pick with here every chance they got whenever Kyra wasn't around or at school. Ari was a target because she was quiet and spent most of her time trying to stay out the way. It was what she was used to. She wasn't scared to fight, she just would rather not. She got hit enough at home and didn't want to have to endure that at school either. She never wanted to get suspended and be left at home for days with her father either. Kyra, on the other hand, had always been Ari's protector. She was the one who stepped up to fight when Ari was pushed into a corner. Kyra was the one who, while Ari was getting hit, came from the side and cleaned whoever was swinging on her.

"Ari'Yonnah is that you with yo ugly ass?!" Cassi the biggest and blackest one of them stepped up and said, *pointing in the car. She knew she had no business calling someone ugly. She always smelled like fried fish and she was so big her shoes leaned to the side. She breathed like she was sleeping, running, jumping and jogging all at the same time. She had on some too short shorts for her to be her size and some cheap ass Dollar Store flip-flops. She had on a $2 white beater and you could see her dirty ass bra straps. It looked like they had never been washed. Ari hated her ass and knew it was going to be some trouble.*

Ari sat quietly and Cassi kept going, "You so fuckin' ugly looking like a cat with them retarded looking eyes."

"Right that bitch's eyes look scary as hell," Tish her sidekick concurred.

They all laughed but Ari didn't think her joke was clever at all, it was really corny. Besides, Tee told her every day how pretty her honey eyes were so she didn't let that bother her at all. Cassi and Tish were haters and Ari knew they were jealous of her. They wished they were as cute as she was and dressed cute like she did. Little did they know if they wanted her life they could have it! Well everything but Tee, he was hers and she wasn't sharing him with anyone. He was the reason she didn't mind waking up every day and the reason she tried her hardest to stay on her daddy's good side so she could see him. She avoided him on occasions, mainly when her daddy would beat her and leave marks on her face. She had heard things about Tee and his family recently scarier than the previous things she'd heard and if any of it was true she knew it was best she kept that part of her life a secret. How could she tell him anyway? She shook the thought from her head when she heard Meka, the girl who had just introduced herself, screaming from the porch.

"Who the fuck is y'all?" Meka asked yelling from the porch down to Cassi and her crew.

"Who the fuck is you?" Cassi shouted back. Ari watched Meka walk off the porch and right up into Cassi's face. Tommy and his uncle had come out the house and two other boys that looked close to our age.

"What's going on out here?" Tommy asked following behind Meka.

"I heard these corny fat hoes out here fuckin' with Ari and I wanna know what's up?!" Meka said motioning for Ari to get out the car. "Get out the car!"

Ari was nervous because she didn't know where this was headed. She took her time getting out the car, pulling down her shirt. She was rocking a purple off-the-shoulder shirt from Express that hung loosely, a pair of black skinny jeans that were also from Express and a cute necklace that hung to the middle of her shirt. She had on a pair of pearl earrings that she'd gotten from Tee and a pearl bracelet to match. Her feet were dressed in a pair of black and silver sandals. She walked out and stood next to Tee.

"I don't know why you tellin' her ugly ass to get out the car for!" Cassi lashed out.

"Right! She scary as fuck!" Tish retorted.

"Y'all got beef with Ari?" Meka asked pulling off her hoodie and standing in just a black beater, "then y'all got beef with me!"

"Girl, you better gon' somewhere, Ari know what it is!" Cassi said rolling her eyes and pointing her black fat index finger in Ari's direction. Her hands were so dry that if she clapped powder would probably fly out or a fire would start.

"Meka its okay" Ari said for two reasons, she would still have to face them at school the next day and because she was not up for a fight.

"You sure?"

"Yes" Ari assured her and it ended just like that.

"Y'all better take y'all asses on and stop fuckin' with my li'l sister!" Meka called out to them as they walked off.

They made it halfway down the street when Tish called out, "Aye Cassi want to fight you Ari'Yonnah."

Pissed and aggravated, something deep down inside told her that was about to happen and when Cassi made it back up the street all eyes were on her.

"I don't want to fight you Cassi" Ari said and meant it. She was bigger than her and she knew Cassi could fight. She'd seen her fight plenty of times. Ari could fight too but she was nervous. She couldn't lose in front of Tee and the *bruises on her sides were still sore from her father's beating a couple days before. Cassi didn't care, she still stood with her arms folded like she wasn't going to budge until she got the fight she was asking for. If Ari went home and had any scratches or anything on her she knew her daddy wouldn't let her out the house for weeks. It was more to this shit than what met the eye.*

"I'll fight you!" Meka agreed stepping in front of Ari.

"I'm still gon' beat Ari's ass!" Cassi said and kicked off her dirty flipflops that still had her footprint in them and posted up, she felt she was finally going to get Ari and if she had to go down the line to do that she would.

Meka beat Cassi up so bad the girls never bothered Ari again, no one did after that actually. They were click tight and wouldn't anything change that.

"I'm not" Meka lied, it wasn't any way in hell that she wasn't about to tell Tommy about this little incident, Meka thought to herself. Ari knew otherwise, as soon as she said she wasn't that it was a lie and soon regretted having told her and not just the other girls. She knew Meka couldn't hold something that they all thought was more serious than it really was from Tee.

"Why you looking at me like that Tammy?" Mia asked and everyone looked up at Meka.

"My bad! Damn, a bitch can't daydream?" she snapped and we all brushed it off.

Meka had been daydreaming a lot and hadn't really been herself lately. Who knew with Meka. Her and her boo might be going through it and you'd never know. She had been acting different that was for sure. Sooner or later she would get pissed and call Ari to vent. Meka hurriedly snatched up her purse and went into the ladies' room while we sat quietly each in their own thoughts when Mia revisited the conversation. "Well I don't feel like you should just brush it off Ari, he could really get dangerous" Mia said with a worried expression planted on her face.

"Yeah bitch he hit you once he a hit you again" Juicy jumped in adding her two cents.

"Well I just think he lost it for a second. I don't think he will actually punch me or anything." Ari half believed the words she'd spoken.

"Just drop it because she pissing me off" Kyra interjected growing madder by the minute.

"Well Kyra what you want me to do, leave him?" Ari asked in a low voice not really expecting an answer.

"Oh, no you don't have to explain yourself to these hoes, you grown now … new subject!" Meka stepped in being the bigger sister as always and reclaimed her seat next to Ari.

Ari always had fun with the ladies, but tonight she couldn't stop thinking about Malik and what he was doing right now.

----> More Than a Friend <----

"This will probably be the hardest thing I will ever have to do, contemplating if some things are better left unsaid"

Chapter 8

Tommy had just finished having a meeting with a few members of his squad when Ari crossed his mind. He hadn't talked to her since that night she stayed at his house and that was about a week ago, so he picked up his cell dialed her number.

"Hello?" a male voice answered and Tommy already knew it was her lame ass boyfriend Malik. Just the sound of his voice changed Tommy's mood. He couldn't let that fuck with him though. Ari was just his friend.

"Yo! Where's Ari?" Tommy questioned him. He'd never understood why Malik felt it was okay to answer shorty's phone, but hey that's the type of shit fuck boys did. Tommy just wanted to hurry and check on her and keep on about his day.

"She's busy who this?" Malik asked knowing damn well who it was. He just wanted to fuck with Ari's so called best friend, just to show him who was boss. He might have had Ari in the past, but it wasn't any doubt that Malik had her right now. At this very moment, she was pissing his cum out her fat cat. Besides he was unsure if she had told him about their little incident from the other night and he wanted to keep her as far away from Tommy as he could so there wouldn't be any problems.

Tommy looked at the phone and decided to play his little game, "this Tommy."

"I'll let her know you called," click.

Tommy looked at the phone again in disbelief. Just knowing that nigga did not just click him. He quickly punched in Meka's number and she picked up on the second ring. Tommy wanted to know why that nigga Malik was acting so weird. He knew he was a bitch made ass nigga but he hadn't ever been this much of a lame. To really hang up on him? He had to laugh a little then he heard Meka's voice.

"What up cuz?" she answered out of breath.

"What you doing that you out of breath with yo fat ass?" he asked not sure he really wanted to know.

"Yeah you don't want to know, what's up though?" she rushed him.

"Have you talked to Ari?" Tommy asked hoping she couldn't hear the concern leaking from his voice. He wasn't used to not talking to Ari on a regular, and he had so much going on within his camp he couldn't believe it had been this long. His money had him distracted and he couldn't believe that her ass hadn't crossed his mind. On top of all that his suspicions were raised even more with their dubious behaviors, Malik on the phone and Ari's sudden disappearance. He was even more pissed thinking about her not calling him either. Like what the fuck was up with that? If she hadn't heard from him then why the fuck hadn't she called? Like what the fuck was really hood?

"She good don't worry, but there is something I wanted to talk to you about," Meka said followed by a dramatic pause.

Tommy knew then something was up and that's why that nigga was acting weird on the phone. He could tell that she didn't want to tell him because she was still quiet. This didn't do shit but pique Tommy's interest even more. He unknowingly ran his hand over the silver diamond encrusted nine that he kept on him at all times.

"Man, what the fuck" Tommy heard Mills say in the background.

"Well, let a nigga know what's good fam" Tommy grew frustrated as he walked into his condo. Tossing his keys on the table he sat waiting for her to start talking again. It obviously was something that he needed to know because she seemed worried to tell him. This for Tommy didn't do anything but raise his suspicions even more. He wanted to know what was up and he wanted to know now. Tommy knew that he needed to keep calm because if he showed her how eager he was she would not tell him.

"Hold on" Meka said and screamed to Mills in the background. "You better chill the fuck out mutha-fucka!"

She got back on the phone and at this point Tommy's blood was boiling. He pushed off his NY snapback rubbing his temple and replaced it when he heard her call for him again.

"Tommy?"

"Yeah and why you cussing so much? Damn be a lady!"

"Shut up. Anyway, it was a situation not too long ago with her and Malik" she started then took another noteworthy pause. Now she was pissing him off, pondering if she should tell him or not. He needed to know what happened and he needed to know now.

"Don't worry cuz, it must be something I need to know and if you tell me I'm sure Ari not gon' be mad at you."

"Don't think you know me" she responded, attempting to laugh her nervousness off, "but he slammed her."

"WHAT?" Tommy exclaimed loudly, more anxious than he had wanted to show to her. His nigga intuition was proved right. He knew something was up with them mutha-fuckas. Furious Tommy just knew he wasn't fucking hearing what the fuck she'd just said to him. She couldn't be fuckin' serious. If she was serious then why the fuck Ari didn't tell him? Clearly seeing the enigma, he started piecing everything together and it all made sense now, her coming to his house in the middle of the night and her not coming around and shit. This mutha-fucka got another thing coming if he thought Tommy mutha-fucking Anderson wasn't going to go see his ass for doing that shit. Right now, he wanted to knock both of their asses the fuck out! He wanted Malik for doing the shit, and Ari's fucking ass for keeping it a fuckin' secret. He low-key wanted to fuck Meka up too cause her manly ass should've called him on site when Ari told her that shit. Tommy hadn't even noticed that he'd knocked his chair back and had damn near worn his area rug out pacing back and forth.

"Just chill, she said he ain't like beat on her, he just kind of picked her up and threw her on the ground."

"I don't care Meka, he shouldn't have touched her!" Tommy was livid. He knew Ari and she didn't deserve that at all. He knew her and her background so he continued to get angrier and angrier. How could he touch her? Tommy thought to himself and talked to Meka long enough for her to talk him out of going over there and killing Malik's ass, but it was cool because Tommy definitely wasn't going to forget. He'd made himself a promise that if Malik's ass did that shit again he would cease to exist and Tommy meant that.

*****

"Who was that baby?" Ari asked Malik as she climbed back on top of him. She had on a cute red and white, lace nighty she'd bought just for him at the sex toy store in the mall. They needed to get back to the place they used to be. She'd been feeling some type of way lately so she was trying her hardest to get them back to their happy place. She no longer wanted to feel like she didn't want to be with him because she did, and she no longer wanted him to feel neglected either. Ari wanted so badly to live and be in love, the lively love that gave her the air to breathe. She didn't want a friendly love that you get and give to friends and family. She wanted to be the air someone breathed and wanted them to be that for her. She wanted the can't go to sleep mad love, the I don't want to be the reason you're sad, love. Ari wanted the finishing each other sentences type of love, the know exactly what you're thinking before you think it type of love. She wanted the communication with only eyes type of love, the you're my number one and only type of love. She felt like if she just tried she could have that with Malik. Maybe that's part of the reason she didn't feel as though she was living.

"Nobody" he said kissing her, getting her hot all over again. They had not sexed this much in one day in a long time. They'd been in the bed together for well over six hours straight. She loved it too. He was taking his time with her and she loved every bit of it.

Ari woke up to Malik gone so she took a shower alone. She made breakfast and got prepared to meet the girls at the hair salon. She hadn't talked to any of them really since the dinner and hadn't talked to Tommy either since the last meeting when she'd stayed at his house that night. She missed him, but maybe it was time for her to grow up and grow out of his comfort zone. Ari slipped on a cute sundress and some cute matching sandals, and pulled up to Elevated Elegance Hair, Beauty and Spa twenty minutes later. Of course, everybody was out. The beauty shop was connected to the barber shop so it was full of people. Ari strutted in and took a seat next to Mia. The next to arrive was Meka, then Juicy and then Kyra. They sat in their little area like always. Ari looked up to see Tommy walk in with a few of his people.

It almost seemed like time stopped when Tommy walked into the salon. His presence alone demanded attention and that's exactly what it got. They all had swag and you could tell they had money just by looking at them. A few were draped in diamonds, a few had on the newest Jay's and all of them were wearing gear from top urban designers. Tommy had on dark green and black army fatigue cargo bottoms, and a black Champs Sweatshirt. He didn't have on any chains, just some iced out 4-carat, princess cut, diamond studs in his ear, and on his wrist rested an iced-out Rolex. Baby looked good.

All the ladies in the shop got quiet and focused on the fine ass Gods who had just blessed them with their presence. The ghetto girls talked louder hoping they would get noticed, and the others tried to play it cool hoping to get noticed as well. All the ladies checked them out. All of them saw something they wanted whether it was money, sex, a baby daddy, something. All of them wanted something from the T.A.A. men as they walked through the salon, catching and holding the attention of all the hungry attention-seeking hoes in there.

"What's up fam?" Tommy said acknowledging the ladies of T.A.A. who were chilling in their own little corner in the salon.

"Hey Tommy" the girls sang, showing respect to one of the men who kept their households running.

"Hey Tee" Ari spoke, continuing to look down, playing Domino on her phone. She didn't want to look at him knowing she had been avoiding him for the past week and a half. She didn't want to look at him but she knew he wouldn't give her any choice. She could feel his intense glare watching her and it had her feeling hot as hell. The effect this man had on Ari was undeniable. She couldn't take him, he was just too much. One minute he was pissing her off, so much so she didn't want to be around him or hear his voice. The next minute she found herself not being able to live without him, her body turned on in places that she'd never even knew she had. Tommy "Tee" fuckin' Anderson had a hold on her.

"Aye let me holla at you Ari."

"Ugh, I knew he was gon' do that," she thought to herself, as she reluctantly rose to her feet and followed him.

Ari was beyond upset with Meka for telling Tommy about what happened. Meka knew Tommy's temper and that he was so quick to fight and shoot. Ari sat listening to him go on and on about her and Malik. She couldn't convince Tee that Malik didn't beat on her. But she came to the conclusion that she wasn't going to fuck with the fam for a while. It was time for her to focus on her relationship with Malik, and the way Tee was talking now made her realize it even more. She knew that living the life she had lived for so long wasn't what she should be doing. She was grown now and not that same little girl who needed T.A.A. to survive. She wasn't existing through them anymore, she wanted to live for herself. She couldn't exist in the world of T.A.A being told who she could and couldn't deal with or trust. Where she could and couldn't go. She dreamed of a time when she could do what she wanted and go where she wanted without having to look over her shoulders, watching her back every minute of the day. It all needed to start with Malik. She wanted to live and build her own family with Malik and live life by his side. She wanted to experience love, happiness, success and growth, and to be proud of it and show it to the world without being afraid someone is going to kill her for it, or someone going to jail for it. She wanted life, without The Anderson family and their associates.

More Than a Friend: The Official, Unofficial Love Story of Ari & Tee

----> More Than a Friend <----

"There's a stranger in my house, it took a while to figure out. You can't be who you say you are, you got to be someone else...."

-Tamia

Chapter 9

"Lemme get two swisher sweets and two blacks" Tommy asked the Arab man working the drive thru. He checked his phone and waited for the man to return.

"That will be five dollars and thirty-five cents" the man said and Tee handed him a five-dollar bill and a single. The man handed back the change and Tommy pulled out of the drive thru store and back into traffic.

"Why you so quiet" Tommy asked while side-eyeing Ari and freaking his mild. He knew exactly why she was acting even more quiet than usual. She knew good and well they always kept in touch, they always made sure each other was good, and for the last week plus she hadn't been and because of that his whole demo was off.

Ari in her own thoughts, honestly didn't know how Tommy would take what she was about to convey to him. For so many years it had been Ari and Tee, ride or die. When she said ride, or die it don't mean she out here in the streets with him slanging and killing people. She's saying she held him down in a way his own momma couldn't. She was his serenity when things stressed him out. She was his cocaine. She drugged him up with her love, and loyalty, taking him to a high that the loudest weed couldn't take him to. She was his addiction whether he admitted it or not. Tommy couldn't get enough of Ari and she him. Their souls were united and that's why it was so hard to tell him what she had to tell him. She knew deep down that either way it went they would always find a way back together, or maybe she wanted it too.

"Tommy, you know we are forever, right?" She asked not really expecting an answer, and not knowing how to let the words escape her mouth. "But it's time I started being a woman and focusing on my relationship with Malik." She couldn't even look his way. She knew him hearing the words she'd spoken was just as hard as it had been for her to speak them. But she needed to say them and he needed to hear them.

"So, what you sayin' shorty? You not gon' fuck with me anymore?" he asked sounding hurt, hoping that's not what she meant. It didn't even sound right. She could only imagine the look in his eyes because she couldn't muster up the courage to actually glance and see. Tee and Ari had been friends for years and she couldn't imagine life without him. She didn't mean she wanted to cut him completely off, and have him out of her life totally. She just wanted to simmer down a little with everything such as meetings, dinners and vacations. She wasn't sure if she could actually *live* without him totally.

"I mean I'll still be here if you need me but I can't keep doing this to him" she continued.

"You act like we fuckin or something, we just friends." He stopped at the red light near the shop and pulled the panties from the mild, tossing it out the window.

"I know Tee, but if I was your girl you wouldn't like me spending so much time with a nigga, would you?" Ari said trying to get him to understand things her way. When she dated Tee as kids he barely wanted her talking to the other niggas in T.A.A. like that so he had to understand where she was coming from. She was always right hand with Tee and it was starting to hinder her from doing what she felt she needed to do as a woman.

"If that's how you want it ma, I ain't gon' fuck ya home up. I'ma always be here though if you need me, like always!"

Tommy got quiet the rest of the ride back to the shop, focusing on his thoughts and concealing his anger brewing inside.

*****

It had been three weeks and Ari hadn't heard from Tommy at all. She hadn't even seen him. She still talked to the girls every day, but even when she was visiting his parents or uncle's he still didn't come around while she was there. She'd stayed away from the meetings and family dinners, but at the end of the day Tommy's family was all she had. Ari refused to cut off mama and the uncles, even if she tried to she couldn't. She didn't mean for it to be like this, but she couldn't stop herself from thinking maybe it was for the better.

Ari was in the yard spraying fertilizer on her plants when the mailman walked up. Her iPod was playing, "Here" by Alessia Cara. She was enjoying herself letting the music guide her.

"Delivery for Ari'Yonnah Childers?" he said startling her, jumping she sprayed fertilizer all over his shirt.

"OMG I am so sorry" she said. "I didn't see you walk up, come in and let me clean that for you."

She invited him in and started to clean his shirt. He was fine and tall with dreads. His uniform did him justice. His skin had turned red from a tan, she guessed it was from walking the neighborhood all day, and his calves were tight. You could tell his job gave him a workout. He also appeared to be married, she spotted the gold band that was located on his ring finger. Ari couldn't help but to check out his sexiness as they conversed. After getting him all clean he walked out as Malik walked up, already looking like he was upset.

"Hey baby" Ari greeted him after shutting the door and saying bye to the delivery man.

Malik stalked over to her as soon as she turned, "Why the fuck was he in my house?"

Ari froze in place thinking of the many directions this could go in. He was pushed up on her so close she could taste his breath in her own mouth. She was nervous and flashes of her father invaded her thoughts clouding her. She was scared.

"Why the *fuck* was he in *my house*?" he yelled causing Ari to flinch.

His voice had raised a few octaves and his chest heaved in and out. Ari couldn't respond she couldn't speak, petrified. He wrapped his big hands, that used to be used for throwing a football, softly around her throat glaring into her eyes. Her silence adding fuel to his fire as he tightened his grip, asking her over and over what the fuck was going on, effortlessly jerking her neck.

"I sprayed fertilizer on him so I cleaned his shirt," She responded to no avail. Releasing her forcefully, her head banging on the front door, he raised his hand in one swift motion and gave her a strong slap.

She ran into the bathroom and locked the door. Sitting on the cold blue and white tile crying, she hoped this wasn't happening again. Everything in Ari wanted to lash out and scream. Malik had her messed up in so many ways. She wasn't up for a fight, not right now, her mind drifting to her best friend. There were only three men she had ever let into her life that she'd really cared about, and now two out of those three had put their hands on her. She couldn't decide if it was worth it, if Malik was worth what could possibly come. She contemplated everything while sitting on the bathroom floor. She knew it was a little dramatic, but she knew that she didn't want to be around him if he thought that was okay.

*****

His palms were sweating knowing that he was one step closer to the person who had ruined his life. He had been tied and tortured and forced to give up everything. He was made to leave everything he had because his *life* depended on it. Do you want to live? Is what they asked when they burned him and cut him deeply. Do you want to live or die? It is your decision. He knew it wasn't his decision because he wanted to live, and the only way to do that was leave everything that he had worked for behind. That wasn't living though. Forced to leave everything you loved behind, everything that you had worked for was existing.

He shook the thought from his mind, trying to forget the pain he had endured for ten days and ten nights until they'd decided they were done and had everything they needed from him. He focused on the new task at hand. He would punish her for causing all his pain and take down everyone she loved and cared about in the process, over the course of ten days and ten nights. She had been tearing him down from the first day he had laid eyes on her, a constant reminder of his failures and where he lacked in life. He managed life with her because she was important to the one he loved the most. The one person who had never judged him, abused him or left him. He looked into her eyes through the T.V. screen and knew it was her.

She had on a long ball gown like they were attending a dinner. She had long, dark black hair and pretty honey eyes. He rewound the news channel he was watching just to make sure he was correct and he was. He knew who she was because she had the eyes of the woman he had loved more than life itself. Her eyes told her story, her pain and now what looked like her happiness.

She was happy for now, but wouldn't be for long. She would soon feel everything he had felt in the last six years. He jerked, his neck twitching, a habit he'd developed after what they did to him. He didn't deserve what they'd done to him for ten days and ten nights. He still remembered it like yesterday. He couldn't help thinking about it every day. Ten days and ten nights, then they dumped him off on the side of the road more than 100 miles from his home, his life. Well 100 miles had dispersed and now he was less than 7 miles away. Malik Johnson, a prospect in training with the Atlanta Falcons had his arms tightly wrapped around her. "Ari'Yonnah Marie Childers," he said out loud to himself, his daughter.

----> More Than a Friend <----

"Fuck bein' friendly, nigga say what's on your mind, naw I'm bein' quiet, I got murder on mine, I got murder on mine, I got murder on mine. Defending what I love, I got murder on mine!

-Kevin Gates

Chapter 10

Tommy had an eerie feeling all day. Something just didn't seem right. He called checking up on everybody in his camp, hesitating when he reached Ari's number. Everything in him wanted to call her but he couldn't. Tommy still couldn't believe that she had basically chosen that lame ass, football playing nigga over him. He still couldn't shake the fact that his gut was telling him something wasn't right. Out here with the life he lived, a gut feeling could be life or death. He'd once had a gut feeling about making a drop with his nigga Los one time.

Tommy and Los had been fucking with some out-of-town niggas and they had been coming through with that bag. Tommy was buying pounds from them niggas dirt cheap, too cheap. He pulled that off using Los as front runner and had those niggas thinking he was a low man, nothing more than a corner boy, who served nickel and dime bags. He had for months put on like he was broke going up under a fake name, Mikey. He even went so far as buying a braided wig and had them niggas thinking he wore his hair in some nappy ass braids. He was planning to meet up with them one day when he had that gut feeling. Ari had called him earlier that day begging him to come chill with her because ole' boy was gone at some football training camp. It was weird because she never made a habit to be that persistent, and she had never invited Tommy over to their place. That's why he respected her so much because she was loyal and when she loved she loved hard. That's how Tommy knew something wasn't right because she always met him at the family's or she'd come to his crib.

When Tommy pulled up to pick up Los he came out like he normally would. As soon as they hit the highway, Ari rang his line. He ignored her call, something he'd never done. It put a nigga in his feelings really quick and deep down inside Tommy thought her voice would ease his weariness.

So, he called her back and she put on that voice, "I need you to come to me now Tee," she exclaimed and he stopped the car on the entrance of the freeway and turned around. Tommy pulled up where he had picked Los up from and told him something had come up and he needed to go now. Los said it was cool, he'd ride up there and front the money and it was okay for Tommy to pay him when he got back. That nigga never came back. He or that money was never found again. Needless to say, when Tommy got to Ari she told him she'd had a bad feeling all day too. She told him she was scared and didn't know why and that's why she had been calling him all day and begging him to come.

"Yo do me a favor and call Ari, make sure she's good" Tommy instructed Meka.

"Ai'ight Tommy" she said sounding annoyed. "But to be honest I'm low-key mad at her cause I haven't talked to her in like a week. If she gon' let that nigga run her then I'm stepping back. Besides, you my fam and I know this shit eating you up, especially after everything we've done for that girl."

"I ain't ask for your opinion, I just asked could you do me that favor" he replied. Tommy was tired of mutha-fuckas giving opinions and shit he ain't ask for. He needed people to do what the fuck he said and when he said it. He had a feeling he was going to have to start putting hot ones in niggas to get shit back on track.

"Yeah I'll call her" she agreed with a lot of attitude before hanging up on him.

Sometimes Tommy wished Meka was not around him all the time growing up because she acted too much like a nigga. They had other cousins, but most of their moms didn't want them hanging with each other. The uncles took care of their children, but their children's moms didn't want the kids around them, mainly T.A.A. The ones who did grow up and decided to come around were given positions, but none like Meka and Tommy. It was always just them two. Tommy walked into his kennel and fed his dogs before letting them out to run loose. Grabbing a beer, he went to the living room and turned to Sports Center.

"Hello?" he answered as soon as his phone rung and Meka's name flashed across the screen.

"She ain't answering, what you want me to do?" she asked her irritation evident across the line. That was a good question, what did he want her to do?

"Nothing, fuck it" he said shrugging his shoulders, and clicked on her like she'd clicked him. She called right back.

"Hang up on me again mutha-fucka" she said and he hung up and chortled.

Tommy called JaMila, this fine bitch he fucked with. He couldn't help but to think that maybe it was time for him to pick a bitch to be his. It had been a minute since he had been locked down and Ari sure didn't seem like she was coming back to him anytime soon. Never would he imagine making a bitch wifey that wasn't worthy of the title. If a broad don't match up something close to the bitches in his squad, then this here wasn't for her. All the niggas he worked with and their bitches were top bitches. Don't get it twisted, all Tommy's hoes were bad but he was more so talking about money motivated. He wasn't trying to build shit with a hoe that couldn't get her own money like Ari did. Ari could get her own money on top of what he tossed her way every now and then. He couldn't help but to shake his head and smile a little, there he was thinking about her again. Mila answered on the second ring.

"I'm on my way" he said not asking, but telling. He hung up, finished his beer and rolled out.

*****

Ari staggered up, dazed and confused off the bathroom floor. Looking in the mirror, she was quickly reminded by Malik's massive hand print on her face. Malik knew she bruised easily and that she was very sensitive. Ari couldn't believe he'd put his hands on her. She cried thinking about what had just happened all over again, pissed at herself for not putting something on her face before a mark showed up. She opened the door hoping he was gone, but he was sitting right in front of the door. She didn't know how or what to feel at this point. What she did know is that if he thought he could put his hands on her then she would be forced to leave. Ari still her own angels on her shoulders, felt that she couldn't say that he's abusive. Hitting her twice from shit that she had instigated really wasn't abuse to her. Abuse to her was how her father had done her. He beat Ari because she was good, he beat her because she was bad, and he beat her because he wanted to. He hated Ari and he beat her for that. That was abuse. She knew abusive personalities and Malik didn't show her that at all. She expected to get snatched up every now and then because she knew she could go there with her mouth when she wanted to. Ari also knew that he was sensitive and sometimes she played on that to get what she wanted.

"Malik" she spoke softly.

"Ari baby I'm so sorry" Malik said as he jumped up and pulled her into him. "I didn't mean to hurt you."

Slightly pushing him away she walked into the bedroom. "I think I'll stay in a room for a couple days" she said starting to pack a bag.

"Baby, please don't leave me" he started to beg.

Ari hated a begging dude. Tee would've never have begged her. Wow, she couldn't help but think to herself. There she was thinking about Tee again. Did I just compare him to Tee? Ari was missing the hell out of him. For a quick second her heart started to race. She hadn't noticed how much she missed him until this very moment.

"I ain't leaving you, but I think you need some time to get whatever's going on with you together! My daddy whooped my ass all my life and I refuse to come here and allow you to!"

"I will never touch you again baby, just stay here!"

Ari wasn't trying to hear him out at all. Maybe it was because she needed some time too. He followed behind her trying to convince her not to leave as she continued to pack. The look on his face showed her everything. He hadn't meant to hurt her and she knew that.

She started to get soft and didn't want to leave him. But she had to, not just for him but for her too.

In the car, Ari contemplated going to Tee's. She hadn't seen him since she'd told him they had to chill and she didn't feel like answering a whole bunch of questions either. What she did know was that no matter how long she went without talking to Tee he would always care for her. He would always come when she wanted or needed him, no matter what. They would be back together like they'd never parted.

Ari called Mia and decided to crash there. She knew Mia wouldn't tell anybody what was going on.

Ari was so exhausted by the time she made it to Mia's she immediately crashed. She was sleep on the couch when Chris walked in at about three in the morning. She heard them talking briefly about her, then moments later she heard moaning. Putting the pillow over her head she forced herself back to sleep, trying not to think about how everything had been going and what she needed to do. She'd been losing herself lately and she didn't know what was up with her.

*****

Tommy had gotten a call last night from Chris telling him Ari was at his crib sleeping on their couch. First thing that popped up in his head was what Meka had told him and the eerie feeling he'd had all yesterday. He got up early and headed there so he could catch her before she left.

Finishing the blunt in the ash tray he cut off the truck and hopped out. He looked around their apartment complex. It was early so no one was outside. The cool air caused his skin to chill even though the sun was shining. He took in a deep breath of it before he knocked on the door. He didn't know what was going on but he was determined to find out. He knocked again and Chris opened the door.

"What up fam," he called out as he walked into their small but comfy home.

"Sup Tommy" Chris replied, doing their gangsta handshake and brotherly hug.

"Hey Tommy" Mia greeted walking up behind Chris, wrapping her lanky arms around him.

"Hey Tee" Ari lifted her head groggily. Her eyes were red and swollen as if she'd been crying and she had a huge slap mark on her face. The slap mark had turned a blueish color and had swelled in a few spots. Tommy instantly got mad and saw red. He just knew this nigga wasn't playing tough with *his* Ari.

"What happened to yo face?" Tommy asked walking up on her and moving her hand. She must've forgotten that she had a mark or maybe she didn't know it looked this bad but it did. Tommy didn't know and didn't care. What he knew was the way his heart was pounding in his chest was slowly causing him to take deeper breaths because breathing right now was feeling really hard to do. The way his trigger finger was itching and the feeling of his gun getting heavier in his waist band, Tommy needed to pull and release a few bullets in Malik's head. Tommy was feeling heavy. His heart was heavy looking at a beaten and bruised Ari. He knew he shouldn't have stayed away from her. This always happened. It happened with her dad and it was happening with Malik. Tommy wanted Ari in every way. He wanted her safe. Ari deserved better and he didn't understand why in the world that was the hardest thing for her to get.

"That nigga put his hands on you?" he asked her. Tommy was waiting to hear what she was going to say, and at the same time his mind was racing so fast that he probably wouldn't hear her even if she'd answered. He didn't realize that he had her chin tightly placed in between his fingers and her head lifted towards him until he felt her warm, wet tears rolling down his hands. His heavy heart was crushed, his baby was not a punching bag and he'd vowed a long time ago that he would protect her from any and every body, and he'd meant it. He didn't care about shit when it came to family he would go to jail for his, but Ari? See, Tommy would die for her!

"Tee" she started, but he cut her off. He didn't want to hear what she had to say or if he was even prepared. The pain from his tightly gripped hands on her chin was causing an odd pain to shoot from the skin, through the gums and her teeth. Tommy was hurting her, but she was willing to endure that pain as long as she was able to stare into his brown eyes, that she'd missed so much.

"Don't Tee me!" he released her and turned to walk out of the house. They must've known he was on his way to pay this nigga a visit.

Tommy didn't know who the fuck Malik thought he was, but he felt like Malik had tried his manhood. Chris was right behind him, and jumped into the passenger seat and they mashed off. Tommy cut his Kevin Gates up and bobbed his head to the music. "Defending what I love, I got murder on mine, fuck bein' friendly, nigga say what's on your mind, naw I'm bein' quiet, I got murder on mine." He listened to "Don't Panic" and retreated into his zone that he had no intentions on letting anybody pull him out of. Tommy lit the mild he'd freaked earlier and continued to push through traffic. Weaving in and out of lanes, he had one mission and that was to set fire to that pussy niggas ass! Bitchass nigga slapped his Ari. Malik had something coming and it wasn't going to be good. Tommy knew if he let Malik get away with it, other corny ass niggas might try him and he wasn't having that, not at all. That wasn't how T.A.A rolled.

In Tommy's world, if a man thought he could get over on you then you risked everything. He would try to infiltrate you and everyone around you. He would try to get your money and anything else you had that he might've wanted. Tommy wasn't that nigga though. He wasn't the type to sit around and wait for the next man, family or not. It was in his blood, the blood that ran through his veins was royalty. It was worth more than gold around this way and he couldn't waste any time on things that didn't build his brand.

He turned onto Ari's and Malik's street and hoped she hadn't given the nigga forewarning he was on his way. He locked eyes on his target and a feeling of relief came over him. Looking into the rearview mirror he saw his eyes were dark.

----> More Than a Friend <----

"God in my heart when I gave back life. I was coolin', I was try'na live a laid-back life.... Real street nigga, no pen to the page, and I will beef with you anywhere, any place."

-Kevin Gates

Chapter 11

Ari hurried off the couch and called Meka on her cell. She'd told her to let Mills know what was happening as she and Mia rushed after Tee and Chris. By the time, Ari and Mia pulled up, Tee and Chris were out the car and Tee was standing toe-to-toe with Malik. "NO!" Ari screamed just in time, running in between them. "Y'all will not do this!" she yelled. Ari couldn't watch the two most important men in her life right now stand out here and tear each other apart. She looked around and observed that her neighbors had made their way onto their porches, and some teenagers had their cameras up ready to film the drama.

"Move back Ari" Tommy said moving her to the side. She saw Danny and Justin pull up and in the car behind them were Juicy, Kyra, and Meka.

"Please don't do this" she pleaded.

"Please don't do this? Look at your face!" Kyra screamed turning everyone's attention towards Ari. She was out the car, high-tailing her way over to the scene.

"Was you screaming please don't do this when he was beating yo ass?"

"Kyra!" Mia screamed.

"Shut up Mia" Meka jumped in.

"Don't tell her to shut up, Ari is a grown woman" Juicy added.

"Y'all all need to chill the fuck out" Danny chimed in. He was the only reasonable man out there trying to help defuse the situation, helping Ari separate the two fuming men.

"Fuck that Tommy! Come on, don't be stupid. Fuck her, let her be stupid if she wants to" Meka fussed, pissed off.

"Meka" Ari cried her tears habituate, flowing down her bruised cheek.

"Nigga I know you ain't come all this way to not do shit!" Chris instigated. Ari shot him the meanest look and Mia told him to shut up.

"Let's leave her alone and let him keep beating her ass, shit let's do what she told you and let her ass be!" Meka continued to rant.

Mills jumped in, "You don't mean that Meka."

"The hell I do" she said before pulling Tommy away from Danny and into his car, driving off.

Ari watched everything take place and cried. Chris and Justin came up to her trying to console her by saying everything would be okay. She barely listened still focused on the street that Tee's truck had just drove down. It wouldn't be and she knew that. They had left her and no one had asked her to go with them. With Tommy and Meka mad at her, she didn't know how she would move on. She sat down in the street crying out. They had really left her; Kyra, Meka, and Tee and not one of them asked her to come, the thought continuously replayed in her head, paining her heart with every beat. She pondered, 'we were *more than just friends.*'

----> More Than a Friend <----

"Fuck bitches and get money!"

Chapter 12

"Damn baby yo shit tight" Tommy said as he pulled out and busted all over JaMila's back. Ever since he'd stopped fucking with Ari and she'd decided to move back in with Malik, shit had changed. He was either working or fucking hoes.

Tommy rolled out the bed, tired from their two-hour fuck session. He needed to relieve some stress. Not having Ari at the meetings had been hard on him. He knew it was because everyone missed her being there. He really missed her, but he had to let her be. Life didn't stop and neither did Tommy. As much as he'd wanted him and Ari to be good they weren't and he had to accept that. Ari had moved on and he had to too. He couldn't let a bitch stop his money flow, not even Ari. He felt this little situation wasn't costing him anything, but to go harder; go harder on building T.A.A., go harder fucking these hoes and go harder getting this money.

He tried not to give a fuck about what was going on over there and to continue on with his life, but he couldn't help thinking about her at times. He loved her with everything and that wasn't going to change. Sometimes Tommy hated the nigga that he was, mainly because he wouldn't hold her ass back from being great. He couldn't do that. Ari deserved the world, even though he did miss fucking her though. All these years later the mere thought of her pussy glistening could make his dick rise to attention.

Tommy glanced back at Mila who had the pillow between her legs looking like she was daydreaming. "What's up ma?" he asked wanting to know what she was thinking and why she was staring through a nigga's soul right now.

"Nothing," she responded turning on her side.

"Naw ma what's good?" he asked her again and she looked at him with sad eyes.

"I just hate to see you leave" she responded.

Tommy really had a soft spot for Mila. Out of all the bitches he fucked on she was the closet one to being anything like his girl. He'd spent time and money on her with no problem. She was beautiful and she had great pussy. He shook his head and crawled next to her, pulling her into his arms, feeling her body instantly relax.

"What you need ma?" he inquired. Tommy was ready to dish out whatever amount she wanted like he had done countless times before.

"I need you Tommy," she answered, looking at him in his eyes. 'Ugh, I hated when she does that it' Tommy thought to himself because it reminded him so much of Ari.

"It ain't about the money, I hate that we can't do stuff together and spend the night together." She stopped talking and he could tell she was in her feelings. "I feel like a side chick" she finished.

"It gotta be a main bitch for you to be a side one baby," he replied kissing her. "I care about you shorty, and that's why I keep our relationship like this. I can't be what you want. I told you from the get-go that I ain't want a relationship and you said you were cool with that. You said, Tommy I just wanna be yo friend."

"How you know if you don't try?" She interjected and looked at him. He couldn't deny her logic.

She was right he could try, Ari wasn't fucking with him so what was holding him back? He started to feel bad for Mila because he knew she was a good girl. He sat in deep thought and came to a conclusion of fuck it. Everybody else was out here living their life and if this is what she wanted, this is what he was going to give her.

"Ok shorty, I can try."

She smiled and kissed him. She moved the pillow and jumped back on top of him, starting another round.

After he left Mila's he headed back to his crib. The entire drive was a blur because the only thing he could think about was the fact that he might have given another bitch Ari's place. But that wasn't possible. No bitch could ever amount to anything close to Ari in his eyes, but then again maybe it was time. He walked into the house tossing his keys on the table and grabbing the remote. He still had a lot on his mind; Mila wanted more and Ari was out of his life but he still couldn't stop thinking about her. He hadn't seen her in a few weeks. He tried not to bring her up, but he felt despondent knowing she didn't have anyone except him and his family. Now that Meka was upset with her also, she hadn't been around. Tommy knew the other girls had been keeping in touch with her, but they'd said she really didn't mess with them anymore. Trying to figure out a way he could see her without it being obvious a brilliant thought crossed his mind. Well, it was brilliant to him at least. He called Danny to see what that nigga was up to.

"What up Tommy" he said on the first ring. "You try'na ride out tonight?"

"I'm down, want me to call up the boys?"

"Yeah do that. Fuck it, I feel like spending so tell the girls to come too."

"Bet."

"Fasho" Tommy said clicking.

Getting up he walked into his closet entrance and tried to figure out what he was going to wear. He knew every time they went out and the girls were with them it would be a nice time. He couldn't help but to think about bringing one of his hoes, but decided against it. His main reason for going out was to see Ari, knowing there was no way her girls was going to go clubbing without her. Besides, he might bring a bitch home, you never know.

Chuckling he grabbed a black Cult Individuality shirt and matching black jeans. He pulled down his black Jordan 11's and grabbed one of his many black G-Shock watches. Knowing he was a fly nigga he had to stay fresh. He went and poured up because he didn't want to go out without a buzz, but he also knew with the whole camp riding he didn't want to be too fucked up. Tommy always had to be in a position to protect what's his.

----> More Than a Friend <----

"Acknowledge: accept or admit the existence or truth of"

Chapter 13

Ari was laid on the couch watching television with Malik. Their relationship hadn't changed and she wasn't living like she thought she would be after separating herself from Tee and T.A.A. Something was missing and deep down inside she knew it was Tee. The void could have easily been mistaken for air or even her heart beat. Everything that seemed to stop, since the day she'd laid in the street and watched his truck speed off. Without Tee, she felt even more depressed than her problems she was still having with Malik. She *still* wasn't feeling their relationship. He'd started being very controlling, always wanting to be up under her or wanted her to be up under him. He repositioned himself when her phone rang.

"Hello" Ari answered low, just above a whisper. It was Mia and she was happy to hear from her.

"Hey chick what you doing tonight?" she inquired sounding very upbeat.

"Nothing, just probably watching t.v. or something."

"Well put yo freak'em dress on 'cus we going out."

"Will Meka be there?" Ari asked not wanting any problems. The last time she'd seen Meka, like Tee, was the day they acted a fool outside her condo. She hadn't heard from either of them or their uncles, and didn't know how they were feeling towards her at the moment.

"Yes, Meka will be there, but I promise I'll keep the peace. We miss you girl" she added making Ari feel bad.

"Okay, I guess."

"Well the only thing is we're taking the trucks and you know the seating arrangements."

"Well can I just meet ya'll there?"

"We're going to Luv and you know how parking is, and we're probably gon' shoot through Jimmy's" Mia added, trying to make Ari realize there was no way she would be able to drive alone because of where those spots were located. Even though she wasn't Tee's girl or anything close to it anymore, she was important to him and everybody knew it. So, she had to be careful. Being from a place were the only thing more valuable to a nigga and his money is his mom's and his girl. So, if you couldn't touch him or his money you went after the next best thing, and you'd have total control over that man himself.

"Well I guess I'll be ready at nine."

Ari got up and started searching for something to wear. She figured she might be able to get someone to switch up the seating order in the trucks once they arrived. Finding a black Chanel dress and hooking it up with some different jewelry, by 9:00 she was downstairs waiting for them to pull up. Ari heard the trucks before she saw them.

When they turned the corner, and stopped by at the curb directly in front of her she opened the door and saw Tee in the driver's seat, Mills and Meka in the second row and Danny and Kyra in the very back. She didn't care how uncomfortable the ride may be, she wanted to be in his presence. She missed Tee and she wanted to be near him right now, even if it was only for a short 25-minute drive.

"Hey everyone" she spoke as she opened the door.

"Hey girlie" Kyra obnoxiously screamed to the front.

"What's up ma" Mills and Danny said in unison.

Ari looked at Tee and Meka and noticed neither one replied as she attempted to hop up in the truck. She was having a hard time because the trucks sat up so high off the ground. They were navy blue Denali's and sat on 26" rims. The bodies of the trucks were lifted a few inches above the tires so that they didn't rub. It was something you drove when you were trying to stunt. The insides of all the trucks were touch screens and had two to three televisions in each row. Ari loved riding in them and was always pissed that Tee wouldn't let her drive one. Another reason they always rode in the trucks as a unit was because they were all bulletproof, right down to the presidential tinted windows. Because of the family's status in the streets they had to be prepared for any and everything.

Ari grew frustrated. She was so used to Tee helping her, and the 6½" Christian Louboutin's on her feet weren't doing any justice to the situation. Little did she know, Tommy was enjoying seeing her struggle to hop in the truck. He loved the stress line that stretched across her beautiful yellow forehead. This moment right now was the very reason he'd even wanted to go out. He wanted to just watch her, to actually see her beautiful face and see for himself that she was good. He took note that she still was gorgeous and didn't have any visual marks that indicated Malik was treating her anything other than what she deserved.

"Maybe this isn't a good idea" Ari sighed about to turn around. She wanted to go out and have fun, but if they were going to act funny towards her she could just stay where she was.

"Girl if you don't get in this car!" Kyra said, most likely agitated at the way Tee and Meka were acting. She would've sent Danny to help if they weren't seated in the far back. She couldn't believe Mills didn't get out and give her a boost. She couldn't help but think that it was because of Meka. She didn't blame Mills, hell who really wanted to deal with Meka's troll ass. She was such a jealous bitch, Kyra couldn't stop her eyes from shooting to the ceiling even thinking about Meka's ways and actions towards Ari. She felt that if Tommy wasn't Meka's cousin she would've probably fucked him years ago; the bitch seems like she's in love with him.

"No, it's okay" Ari said on the verge of tears. She always hated that she cried when she was frustrated, and right now she was very frustrated. The man who had always been by her side was treating her like she was another bitch on the street who meant nothing to him, and the bitch she always felt was a sister to her was treating her even worse.

"Man" Tee mumbled under his breath as he got out the truck and helped her in like he used to.

He returned to the driver's seat and sped off. Ari sat quietly the whole time, stealing a glance or two of Tee. Little did she know he was doing the same thing as Meka watched from the backseat scowling. She did not want Ari to come. She looked at Tommy and just wished that this didn't set him back. When they arrived to the club they walked straight in and up to the bar. Opening a tab, they all started to drink. It was so nice in Luv and everyone enjoyed going there. It was always packed and it gave Ari a chance to see everyone she'd known back when she was in school. Most of them was tore down but hey, you couldn't fault anyone for the things they'd went through as kids. You had to want to do better in order to be something in life. She was motivated and she had Tee, but everybody didn't have a Tee they could count on.

*****

"Who can I run to, to share this empty space? Who can I run to, when I need love? Who can I run to, to fill this empty space with laughter? Who can I run to?"

-Xscape

Ari was enjoying the night out, but she was still in her feelings. Tee and Meka wouldn't look her way. Kyra pulled Ari onto the dance floor and started dancing wild. She wanted to make her girl feel better, and keep her mind off of the way that Tommy and Meka were acting. She peeped it all and knew that it had to be eating Ari up. Kyra knew her friend like she knew her own self and one thing she knew was Ari didn't want any problems. Kyra knew that if Ari started to feel some way she would distance herself from everyone and that's the last thing any of them needed. Kyra never wanted her friend to feel alone like she'd been in the past; and most importantly she damn sure didn't want her to cut everyone off and that nigga Malik think he could have her and do her however he wanted to. Not on Kyra's watch.

Ari, laughing and clowning with Kyra tried to keep her mind on just having a nice time tonight, drama free. Two guys walked up on them and wrapped their arms around Ari and Kyra, so they could dance with them. The girls were dancing and having fun when Ari's partner started to get too touchy-feely, trying to pry his hands off he was too strong. Ari completely stopped dancing and he still was trying to bend her over. Kyra had disappeared into the crowd and as Ari struggled to wiggle away from him she looked up to the VIP area and saw Tee watching everything that was going on. She could see his jaw clenching from afar. He walked away and that crushed her. She knew he could tell that this dude had taken the dancing too far. Where was the rescuer who'd always saved her?

Tee stood and watched ole boy feel Ari up. It took everything out of him not to walk down and sleep his ass. He patted his loyal nine that he kept on him at all times, considering it. He didn't want to shoot this bitch up, so he decided to just let her be like she requested. He walked over and started chatting with Mila, who just happened to be at the club.

Ari couldn't stomach the fact he didn't walk down and put this aggressive dude in his place like he used too. It had always been like that with Tee, which was one of the main reasons they'd become best friends. They had always been drawn together and he'd always had her back. Tee always felt the need to protect Ari and keep her safe. Ari didn't feel any differently now, and she knew he was hurting and he didn't know how to handle that. Loyalty was one of his family's mottos and they all lived by it.

Ari finally managed to break free of the guy and made it back upstairs with Kyra and Mia. Relieved, she sat at the bar when she noticed Tee talking to a cute girl. Catching herself staring at them and the way he was touching her made Ari emotional. She felt herself getting jealous as the girl smiled and giggled at whatever he was saying to her. She moved in closer and wrapped her arms around his neck, as he placed his hands on her ass. Ari grew angry as she watched them and yet she couldn't tear her eyes away. This was the first time she had ever seen him with another girl like this, ever. She had seen a few girls he messed with and he seemed to always blow them off when he was with or around Ari, but with this girl something was different. Ari could tell that they were into each other, she could see that Tee was into this girl and Ari's heart was officially broken.

"You good?" Kyra asked, snapping her from her daze.

"Yes, why you ask me that?" she couldn't sound any less dejected even if she tried, as she sipped from a little bottle of Moscato.

"Bitch you been MIA and shit. I ain't used to that," Kyra responded sipping her drink too. Ari and Kyra both looked up to see a drunken Meka stumble over to Tee. Across the room, even though Tommy tried hard to focus on Mila he couldn't until he saw Ari take her seat with Kyra and Mia.

He had mentally given her 3 ½ minutes to get upstairs, or he was going to go down and fuck that drunk, aggressive ass nigga all the way up. He was able to relax a little when he saw her and their eyes locked. He on the low watched her watch him and Mila. Usually, he would've kept it cool in the club and definitely in front of Ari, but something in him wanted to make her jealous. He wanted her to feel the way he felt every time he saw her with Malik. He wanted her to feel how hurt it was to not talk to her every day. He wanted her to think that he didn't need her anymore and that it was many more women out there who would die to be in her spot. There were plenty of women out there who would love to have Tee, and Mila was one. He wanted Ari to hurt and be jealous. So, he put on a show, that is until a drunken Meka stumbled over to him.

"You good cuz' fuck her" she said rolling her eyes, sloppily pointing in Ari's direction. He could tell she'd had way too much to drink. She was sweating and he could barely make out what she was even saying.

"Just chill Meka talking like that bout her" Tommy said not knowing why he was defending her. He figured it was just natural.

"Mila I'll holla at you later." he dismissed her because Meka was drunk and continued to talk.

"You my fuckin' cousin and if you hurt I'm hurt, and that bitch got you hurting after everything we've done for her" she said loudly and tapping on her chest hard that you could actually hear it.

"Chill Meka! Fuckin' putting my business in the street, da fuck wrong wit' you?" he said sternly, but never raising his voice. His tone alone had her shaken up, as he tried to get her to quiet down, but the liquor had taken over.

"Naw don't tell me to chill, I oughta go tap dat hoe."

Tommy knew she was only acting like that because she missed the hell out of Ari too. He knew Meka and she wasn't much without her right-hand Ari. Even though Meka was the older sister she talked to Ari about everything, shit he didn't even know about and didn't find out about until months later.

"Naw Meka you drunk, you don't wanna do dat." He tried to convince her and trying figure out how many drinks she'd actually had. He usually watches everything and he hadn't even seen her drink that much. Besides, she had been in and out the bathroom so much he figured she would've peed everything out.

"You pissing me off Tommy, why do you care about her so much? Huh? You act like you love her more than you love me!" her voice screeched and she started crying.

"It's time to go" Tommy shifted and signaled for the boys.

"You not gon' even tell me that ain't true Tommy? Damn that's fucked up." She was riding an emotional rollercoaster, her tears flowing down her cheeks and nose running.

Tommy was so upset with her for acting out. He knew it was the liquor, but still she didn't have to cut up. He looked over and saw Ari gathering her things, finishing up her drink after Danny approached them. She looked so good in her little black dress. She always looked good, he had to admit she had it going on.

"Come on y'all we out" Tommy said letting everybody know what time it was, making sure his team knew what the fuck was going on.

Meka had walked off and Tommy heard her yell "bitch" as she charged at Ari. He couldn't believe that she would let the liquor take her over like that, getting her to the point she wanted to fight her. Kyra stepped in front, stopping her in her tracks. By this time, Ari was standing up with her purse in her hand. Tommy, finally made his way over, snatched Meka up by the arm jerking her harder than he'd meant to. He was so upset with her he couldn't control himself. Everybody knew that Ari was his soft spot and everybody knew that he would never let anyone cause her harm. Everybody knew that and Meka knew that now also. He didn't care who it was. He loved Meka like his sister, and yes, they are blood related, but this was Ari. *His* Ari.

"Are you seriously trying to fight me?" Ari asked shocked with pain written all over her face.

"Fuck you bitch, you ain't shit!" Meka screamed at her. "You wouldn't be shit if Tommy wasn't there for you, MY FAMILY MADE YOU!" she continued.

With all eyes on his squad, Tommy gave the nod to one of his people to let them know shit was cool. Tommy being the man he was always had people around who were willing to die for him and he paid them well for that. He always had some hitters waiting, and watching making sure he was safe and that anybody that he rolled with was.

"Chill the fuck out Ta'Meka!" he screamed at her, shaking her like a rag doll. Mills grabbed her from Tommy, shaking his head. Mills was tired of Meka himself, but he couldn't let Tommy do her any kind of way. He himself wanted to defuse the situation before it got out of hand. He knew like everyone else in their squad knew

Tommy loved Meka, Tommy loved Ari and to see this taking place threw him off his hook-up. It could be way worse than what meets the eye. Only true ganstas knew that.

"Forreal Meka?" Ari wailed now in tears. "Sorry but those were the cards I was dealt!" Ari yelled back, turning and rushing down the VIP stairs. Kyra and Meka started to argue and the other girls stood and watched. The fellas stood between them trying to calm the situation. Tommy, being Tommy went after Ari, but she wasn't anywhere to be found.

----> More Than a Friend <----

"I'm not gon' cry, I'm not gon' shed no tears!"

Chapter 14

Ari was pissed and the tears flowed freely from her eyes. She walked into the bathroom trying to gather her composure, calling Malik at the same time. He picked up on the first ring, "What's up?"

"I need you to come get me."

She was feeling the wine and tried to explain everything, crying all at the same time. Ari couldn't believe Meka had really tried to fight her, she broke down even more. How could she do that to me? She didn't understand how they'd gotten that bad. There'd been a point in time when she'd beat girls up for trying to fight Ari, and now she was out here against her. Ari's heart was hurting and she could hardly think straight, as she hung up and walked outside into the night air. It really was a beautiful night that had turned very ugly for her.

"Aye ma you good?" Ari heard a voice say and she turned to see a gun pointed in her face. "Run that shit bitch!"

"I don't have anything!" she protested with her hands up.

"Give me your purse and that necklace!" he said and she hurried and gave them up.

"Come on B niggas startin' to come out, let's ride!" another voice yell from a black 2007 Dodge Neon.

She watched the dude with the gun turn and jog over to the waiting vehicle, breaking down again, she cried harder this time. She was so distraught that she didn't know if she should run, stay or what. She decided to just wait. She no longer had a phone, and everything was in that purse.

When Malik picked her up she sat in the car crying, half listening to him tell her he'd told her so. She had just been dogged by the people she thought were her family and robbed while she waited for him to pick her up. All she felt at this point was how she needed change and maybe it started with not being around the family anymore, and that included Kyra. Malik and Ari sat in the car and discussed calling the police to report the robbery, but it didn't make sense because none of the things taken were worth anything to fuss over. She could buy another phone and purse, the only thing that had meant something was the necklace because it was a gift from Tee. But she figured it would be pawned off by the morning anyway. Looking out the window in deep thought, crying as Malik held her, she was back alone again and felt like the day she'd lost her mother. Her heart burned as the images of Tee's arms wrapped around that beautiful girl invaded her thoughts once again. Maybe this was an eye opener for her not to be around them anymore. They clearly didn't need her anymore. They were all living life without her, Tee was living life without her. Maybe this is the Lord's way of telling her life would be better without any of them and giving her this final night to show her just that. She would be able to live life without them.

*****

Tommy walked into the meeting with his team already in a bad mood. Shit had been coming up missing and he was out of a few stacks. He didn't want to, but if he had to kill one of these niggas as an example he would. His hands were itching for it anyway. His uncles were trying postpone the advancement because of this, as if these few thousand dollars were really big enough to stop them from retiring. Either way it goes, Tommy wasn't going to let his promotion be compromised because these corny ass niggas wanted to play pussy with his mutha-fuckin money.

Glancing at his phone, he slipped it into his pocket. Ari hadn't gotten in touch with anyone since the other night and her phone was going straight to voicemail. Kyra called Tommy earlier telling him how she'd gone to visit her and that nigga wouldn't let her in. Tommy started to shake his head thinking about it all over again, pussy ass nigga. And here again she was on his mind when his mind should've been on his money. It seemed as if the farther they were from each other the harder it was from him to focus. All these years he'd kept their relationship platonic not only because that's what she wanted, but because that was the only way he felt like he could protect her. Tommy knew that he was a young, boss nigga with money and he loved the attention that the hoes gave him. He knew niggas were

More Than a Friend: The Official, Unofficial Love Story of Ari & Tee

always in the corner plotting on him and his crew, so not having her around was best. He knew that he couldn't be the nigga that Ari deserved, so if being her best friend would keep her with him and safe, then that's what he was willing to do. But now it seemed like he couldn't protect her or her feelings anymore, and that alone set a nigga's balance off.

"Which one of y'all bitch niggas coming up short on dough?!" he asked authoritatively.

The room was filled with only five niggas other than his main ones. They were all part of the same camp, and when they delivered it was always short. Tommy really would hate to punish them all for one weak link, so he was talking to them too. He only fucked with these niggas to a certain extent when it came to his money. He couldn't have any dummies on his team because this was life or death. Everybody waited for Tommy to stop venting before they all tried to explain at once.

"Fuck what y'all saying, next nigga come up short catching a bullet to the brain" He said before turning and walking out.

Leaving and driving around checking on his blocks and different traps, making sure everything was running smoothly, he had to make sure everything was cooking because he couldn't go off word anymore. He'd started thinking of ways to invest his money so he could live a little better than he was. He could have the cars but the houses brought the questions, and until he was able to answer those he would be stuck in the condo he was already in. His uncles and father were trailblazers, they'd help get you started, but felt everyone should make their own way. So, they helped to a certain extent but felt he was a man now and he would have to find what was for him. He understood that, and that's what made him stronger in a way. Everyone thought that he was given his position but in reality, he worked just as hard, maybe harder than anyone in T.A.A. They showed him no love when it came to business he had to make his own name to the higher ups, name dropping didn't work. That's why he'd decided he was going to keep a close eye on these fools because they were getting comfortable. He was starting to believe his camp was a little too big and maybe it was time for him to downsize. He had dreams of taking T.A.A. to a whole different level. He smiled a sly smile knowing exactly how he was going to do it. Picking up the phone he dialed QB's number.

QB was a general from another camp, but he was more like family so Tommy hung with him a lot also. They got real money together and he was someone Tommy could say he honestly trusted. QB was the only person who knew Tommy like Ari knew him, and he had the same morals, mindset, and goals, especially when it came to money. QB and Tommy had killed a few niggas together and were the only two who knew. Tommy would take everything the two did together to his grave and he knew for sure QB would do the same. Their mothers were close, so they took their brotherly relationship serious. Sooner or later they'd be the only two left when it was time for Tommy's uncles and dad to lie down. In the game, everyone eventually did.

----> More Than a Friend <----

"I will always be his lady"

Chapter 15

"Hello?" Ari answered surprised. Her phone never rang unless it was Malik. She'd gotten a new phone and number ever since the robbery. Malik walked into the kitchen and stood next to her while she took the call and cooked dinner. He wanted to know who was on the phone also and wished it wasn't anyone from her old life. He loved the time they were spending together, he was finally getting her to how he wanted to her to be. Who knew all he needed to do was get them thugs out her life to see just how fragile she was. She was easy to manipulate and he loved that. She did whatever he wanted when he wanted her to. That smart mouth and snappy attitude all went out the door the minute they finally got out her life. He loved the fact that he had her all to himself and now she knew she had no one but him it was just that much sweeter.

"Hey Ari'Yonnah" a male voice boomed through the speaker.

"Oh, hey Uncle Tevin" Ari recognized it was Tommy's uncle. It was crazy how just the sound of his voice made her melt. Uncle Tevin, the biggest boss, always treated Ari like a daughter. Oddly enough being the one who was feared the most, he was the one who made her feel the safest other than Tee.

"Well I was calling you because we need you to come to dinner tonight. Don't worry it's not a meeting, it will be strictly dinner. Wear Navy blue, black, or white and make sure you're here at eight" he requested.

Ari glanced at the time and saw that it was already 6:30. "Well Uncle Tevin I don't know if you know, but I no longer speak with Tommy and Meka" she said knowing he already knew. There wasn't too much the uncles didn't know.

"That's not what I asked. Now, you need to be here at 8:00 okay?" he replied making sure Ari understood him. There was no turning down the uncles. She agreed and figured if she rushed the food she could be ready by that time. Already preparing herself because she knew Malik wouldn't like the fact that she was going, Ari sighed and ended the call.

*****

"You are not fucking going!" he said raising his voice. "I thought you left them mutha-fuckas alone!" Ari felt that ever since he'd been released from training camp he had not been the best person to be around and wanted to be up under her 24/7. He had been working small gigs for sports center and the little sports stations around the city, but not being on the field was changing him.

"Well there's nothing I can do, I have to go and I have no choice."

Putting on her earrings and stepping back to look at the dress she'd chosen, she smiled. She had on a navy-blue slouch dress that hung loosely off one shoulder and a pair of black and navy Red Bottoms. She didn't want to wear too much make-up so she darkened her eyebrows and did a little silver eyeshadow. Happy it was just dinner and not a meeting, Ari didn't have the energy to attend a meeting and didn't want to be gone that long. Ari couldn't help but think about the last time she had seen everyone and the girl that Tee was with. She didn't know how she would feel if the girl was to be at dinner. Where would she sit? Ari always took her place next to Tee, if he gets a girl would she be replaced? Her stomach turned and for a quick second she felt nauseous. Then she thought about how pretty she looked and knew that it didn't matter. She was still his Ari and she knew that deep down inside Tee would always love her. She would always be his lady.

"You're so stupid" Malik walked, pissing Ari off.

"How am I stupid, please enlighten me?!" she snapped without giving him a chance to answer. "I swear, now that you don't have football anymore you walking around here all sappy like a fuckin' 8-year old girl who lost her puppy." Before she could stop herself she'd already jumped in his face. "You weren't good enough, let that shit go and get a real fuckin' job!" Ari covered her mouth and the look in his eyes was dark. She hadn't meant to take it that far.

"What should I do, huh? Sell drugs like your best friend?" he mocked using his hands to make quotations around the word best friend. "You know what Ari'Yonnah, go run to them mutha- fuckas like you always do!"

He was hurt and couldn't believe that she had said that. All Malik ever wanted from her was for her to love him like he knew she loved them. He wanted to be important to her like they were. He wanted her and the only way he felt like he had her is when he was controlling her. What he wouldn't do is stand around and be disrespected like he did anything other than love her. Ari knowing, she went too far, grabbed his arm as he started to walk away and with one forceful, swift movement he pushed her off of him. She flew across the room, unable to catch her balance smashing into the mirror and shattered glass went everywhere. Blood was now dripping from her eyebrow. They hadn't had an incident since Tee had come to lay the law down on him. He'd clearly lost his mind. He was making it really hard for Ari to prove that he didn't beat on her and that they had simple fights like any other couple.

"Malik!" Ari cried, trying to brush the glass off her but there were pieces still stuck in the cuts she'd gotten.

She grabbed her purse and dialed Mia as she quickly exited the condo. When she answered, Ari politely asked if she could remove some glass shards from her eye. When Ari arrived at her place she didn't say much as she removed the small pieces of glass. Fixing herself to the best of her ability, Ari thanked her and continued on to Uncle Tevin's.

By the time, she arrived it was 8:30, which wasn't good. They were sticklers for promptness and as she strutted into the dining area all eyes were on her. She could tell by everyone's facial expression what they were thinking, but she didn't care about that right now. She was happy to see that her seat was empty and Tee was looking as handsome as ever. He was in a navy-blue button up and he had on a princess cut diamond chain and a diamond Rolex that she could see glistening from where she was standing. He had two princess cut diamond earrings resting comfortably in his ear. He looked at Ari, and with just a gaze he caused her to heart race, and her panties to moisten. Flooded with different emotions she missed him.

She walked around and spoke to everyone then took her seat by Tommy. They didn't say a word to each other. After they were done eating Uncle Tevin passed out envelopes to certain people. She opened hers and inside was $1500. She thanked him, knowing it was her allowance she didn't feel bad for accepting it. When everyone began to chat, she mingled with a few people, but still not with Meka or Tee. Feeling the tension, she was uncomfortable. Everyone around could sense it, being they are all normally stuck at each other's hip. When she was ready to go, she excused herself.

QB tapped Ari lightly as she slowly tried to leave. He was one of Tommy's homeboys and ran a camp of his own. He always came to the meetings alone though. She was starting to think he was gay because she'd never seen him with a girl out of all the years she'd known him.

"Aye, where you been?" he asked pulling her into a tight, brotherly hug and kissed her cheek.

"I been around. You?" she smiled.

"Good. Good. Same thing different day. Just moved in with my old lady and hopefully y'all will meet soon," he said. That killed her thought of him being gay, well she would have to see it for herself though. She knew he was just making conversation but she was drained and ready to get up out of there. She couldn't take any more of the awkwardness.

"You sure you good sis?" he touched the knot above her eye softly. One thing she did know is he's just as crazy as Tommy, so she would never tell him she wasn't.

"I'm good bro, I promise!" He said ai'ight and she turned and headed out the door. Ari heard someone scream out for her to wait.

"Hey" she said low, not really in the mood to talk to Meka.

"Pooh I'm so sorry for everything that happened" Meka started. "I know I was wrong but look at you" she cried, touching Ari's face delicately.

"I'm sorry too" Ari replied turning to walk away. She wasn't sorry for anything she'd done she was simply sorry for Meka's mistake, and for that they couldn't be cool in her eyes. "but don't worry 'bout me, I'm fine."

"Wait!" she said stopping Ari again, "I want us to be like we used to be" she said sniffing. "I miss you sis and I'm dying just looking at you right now."

"Why? I told you I'm cool."

"Look at your face, you are not cool Ari" she said getting upset. "Look at how he is treating you."

"Don't worry about me, I'm fine really. Look, I have to go but just give me a call later okay?" Ari said trying to hurry home. She was done with this conversation and didn't want them to think they were cool just because she showed up here tonight. She still needed her space to figure things out for herself. She didn't want to make Malik more upset than she knew he already was so right now she wasn't going to do this. She wasn't going to cry in each other's arms like they were good and forget about things that happened. Meka tried to fight her, got her robbed and that alone was something that she wasn't ready to get over yet.

"Okay I will" she agreed then walked back towards the house.

----> More Than a Friend <----

"Gotta get shit back right by any means necessary, with all means necessary"

Chapter 16

Tommy upset sitting and talking with the Uncles. Yes, he knew that nigga Malik was playing tough guy. Yes, he knew that Ari was going through hell and no, he hadn't done anything about it. Pride wouldn't let him. He tried to convince himself that it wasn't happening more times that he even wanted to admit to himself.

"You need to step in before he kills her" Uncle Tevin said. He had a soft spot for Ari and everyone knew it. Maybe it's because they're Capricorns or something, being they're birthdays were only days apart.

"You know what we have to do" Tommy's dad stated rhetorically. He always wanted to go straight for the jugular. He knew his pops was a killer, and that was always his first choice.

"I know man, but that's her choice. She told me to leave her alone" Tommy responded knowing he sounded like a female.

"You're just going to let her go?" Uncle Tevin inquired.

"Look I gotta go" Tommy irritated raised from his seat, preparing to leave.

QB had pulled him to the side before he left, telling Tommy about some work he needed to put in before they went to handle business that night. Tommy knew what that meant after he'd said it, they had to lay somebody down. Sure enough, this new bitch he'd been fucking was getting shitted on by her mom's or some shit, so we had to lay her down and her nigga too. It was cool with Tommy because he himself showed no love to anyone when it came to Ari, so he knew QB loved his shorty if he was willing to put her mom's down. One thing he knew about QB was that nigga's crazy was on another level. Uncle Tevin snapped Tommy out of his train of thought.

"Well, I'ma call her tomorrow and you're going to bring her back here." Uncle Tevin demanded.

"Why can't she drive?"

"Because it seems like she can't make it on time. Don't ask questions Thomas" Tommy's dad interjected in an authoritative tone, his voice roaring.

"Ai'ight man," Tommy walked to the hall and stood there pulling out his keys to leave when he heard Uncle Tevin and his pops talking.

"Every time I look at her she puts me in the mind of Tamera."

"Don't you speak that name!" he heard his dad barked.

"She's your daughter Thomas!" Uncle Tevin retorted and continued. "She's going through a lot right now and I'm trying my hardest to support her since you can't man up and do it!"

"You shouldn't have murdered that doctor, he was keeping her together because her slut of a mother sure couldn't!" Uncle Tyson added.

"I don't want to talk about it!" Tommy heard his dad say and then heard muffled sounds as if he was coming through the door.

Tommy walked away, making a mental note to look into exactly what they were speaking on. So far it sounded to him like he had a long-lost sister that he didn't know about. This was something serious to him and everything he believed and was taught.

He was in a mood to kill somebody. He couldn't believe that nigga Malik really be beating on his Ari, and on top of that he might have a sister somewhere out there he didn't know about. He sat in his car and began to think of a master plan. There was a lot of shit going on around him and it was time to put a straightener on it. He had a feeling things were probably about to get out of hand and he had to make sure his cards were in place when they did. For starters, what could he do to get Ari back in his corner?

*****

Tommy finished rolling a blunt and bobbed his head to Kevin Gates as QB and him cruised through traffic.

"So, when I'ma meet yo lady shorty?" he asked his brother from another mother blazing up.

"Soon, I mean we just getting locked in so I'm try'na see where her head at," he paused and took a drag off the blunt Tommy handed him. "I mean she ain't bout this life son! I'm try'na keep her from this shit for real."

Tommy felt every word he'd said because that's how he felt about Ari. They said they were best friends and all that, but deep down inside she's always going to be his leading lady. He just needed her to realize that.

"I can dig that," Tommy sat back and listened as QB continued his thoughts.

"I mean her mom's a piece of shit and I'm done with her! She embarrassed her and threw her out and all the neighbors was watching and shit," he stated shaking his head and Tommy could see the hurt plastered on his face. He also knew it was more to the story on why he wanted to off her, but it wasn't his place to ask. He always going to ride for his brother, no questions asked.

QB and Tommy pulled up to a nice two-story crib in the suburbs. All the lights were out and they already knew what to do step-by-step. QB pulled off and Tommy ran through the yard to the garage. It was easy to remember the garage code because it was the year he was born. When it opened, he hurried and shut it and found a little spot to chill when the garage door started to open right back up. He knocked a few things down with a crash trying to fit deeper between the little spaces so couple wouldn't see him and pull off. As soon as he was secured the car started to slowly pull into the driveway. It was bad to have smoked that blunt because it had me paranoid. He mustered up his gangsta and pulled his strap. A black Ford Fusion pulled into the garage and stopped. He could see it was two people in the car and as soon as the garage shut and the car door opened he grabbed the driver and put the chromed 9mm to his head. Tommy didn't bother to mask up because they weren't going to live to point any fingers.

"Pop the trunk bitch or I'ma shoot this nigga in the head!" Tommy said and the woman froze in place. "Don't scream either or I'll shoot you too!"

She hurriedly popped the trunk and stood next to it staring at Tommy. He didn't know if it was the weed or not, but he was feeling some type of way. The bitch was too calm and almost seemed like she was familiar with him or something. She didn't seem scared like most bitches would've been. High he chalked it up to she might've been hip to game.

"Get in bitch and hurry up!" She hesitated but got in. Tommy walked dude over to the trunk and pushed him in on top of her. "My man what you want, what we do?!" He questioned with his hands up crying like a bitch. "You gon' find out soon, we about to take a ride!" Tommy replied and started to shut the trunk when she spoke.

"Tell him I'm sorry and I never meant to hurt y'all!" Taken by surprise, Tommy was confused about what she was speaking on. Shutting the trunk, he hopped into the driver's seat of the Fusion and hit the garage door. He backed out, hit it again and flashed QB to follow after him. It didn't take long to reach the warehouse district. QB parked the stolen car they drove there, up the street just in case the cameras were watching and hopped in the car with Tommy. They searched for Lot 27 garage B storage units, as they whipped through the storage lot. After they got the couple out the trunk, neither put up a fight. QB and Tommy both walked one to each side of the car, and put them back in the front seats. QB shot them up with some liquid behind the ears and they were out. Both men masked up as Tommy shut the storage unit and they jogged up the street until they made it to the stolen car. Tommy didn't relax until they were in the city.

*****

"Okay Malik I really don't care," Ari and him were fighting again.

She couldn't understand, what part of "I can't disrespect the uncles when they give me orders" didn't *he* understand? They felt like orders, but were more like requests. They had done a lot for Ari and gotten her out of a bad situation; they'd handled her father and let her move in with them until she'd finished school and made sure she was good all the way around, mentally, physically, financially and emotionally. Ari had been through a lot and they'd been there every step of the way. Uncle Tevin had given her the run down on men when she'd gotten her heart broken by her first boyfriend, which was Tee of course. Ari knew it was hard for him to do, but he ran down the game to her, even though it was his nephew, just like he'd run down the game to Meka years before. He'd helped Ari grow as a woman and was the daddy she'd never had. Tee's dad was there too, but they hadn't had the same relationship as Ari did with the uncles.

She totally blocked out everything Malik had said in the past few minutes, lost in her thoughts. He didn't realize they didn't take kindly to people who didn't listen to them or who went against the grain.

"You think I'm playing, you're not going!" he said jumping in her face.

"Yes, I am" she said defiantly.

Malik pulled Ari and slammed her on the ground. He couldn't control his anger knowing that every time she went around her old friends he was losing her again. He wanted her and wanted her only to want and need him. For Ari, this was not good, and she felt like she was falling back into her past. She had flashbacks every now and then about her father and the awful beatings he used to give her. She heard a knock at the front door and fear consumed her, already knowing who it was. Tee always picked her up at the door unless she was already downstairs waiting for him. Who knows how many times he had probably called her phone within the past couple of minute while her and Malik had their dispute.

"Who is it?" Malik yelled out still grasping a fistful of Ari's hair.

"Please Malik let me go!" she bellowed, fighting to stand up.

He let her go and watched as she staggered to her feet before he opened the door. Tee stood at the door in an all-black Polo sweat suit and some wheat Timberland boots. His cologne permeated through the air and invaded her nostrils instantly calming her.

"You good?" he asked looking at Ari for any sign that she wasn't. He wanted her to say she wasn't deep inside because he already had his hand tightly gripped on his nine that was resting in the pocket of his hoodie. He gripped it the minute he heard Malik's voice when he knocked. He wanted so badly to knock this nigga down, but for the love of Ari it wouldn't be today.

Ari was put back together, but she was sure her skin was still flustered. "Yes, Tee let's just go" she said trying to fix herself completely. It was still odd to be around the two of them and prayed they wouldn't try to attack each other. She just wanted to get away from Malik, but she also wasn't prepared for a car ride with Tee. She hadn't said hardly any words to him in so many weeks. She honestly didn't know how to feel.

Tee didn't say anything else, but Ari could read what he was thinking on his face. She didn't know how she'd ended up like this. She thought about how it was her only way of life before Tee had entered it, but now it was back to before. Tee was the only man in her life that had never hurt her physically, the only man that had never even raised his hands to her.

----> More Than a Friend <----

"I'm so tired of tears"

Chapter 17

Ari cried as the cool night breeze blew across her skin. It was the middle of June so the summer rush was just beginning. Usually you would see a few people sitting out late on a night like this, but tonight there was none. It was only Ari out here at four in the morning, standing at Tee's door. Another really bad argument between her and Malik, and the look in his eyes had her feeling like she needed to run before shit got uglier than it already had. She wasn't too fazed by him grabbing her up, but what he'd said to her put a strain on how she viewed him, the way he went about it. She'd left having nowhere else to go and went to the only sane safe place she'd ever had. She hadn't talked to any of the girls or any other member of T.A.A, so it would've been odd to just show up at their doors. Even with the silent drive to visit the uncles and the silent drive home she didn't know where she stood with Tee but; here. She knew she was always welcomed, no matter what. Using her key to walk in, everything was neat as always. She fumbled for the light but had too much stuff in her hands, causing a loud crash. The lights flicked on and Tee was standing there with his gun aimed towards her.

"Damn Tee how many times you gon' pull that out on me?" Ari asked trying to laugh off her nervousness. It had been months since they'd had a real conversation. They hadn't talked, even while they were at the uncles. As of now they were strangers.

"What are you doing here Ari?" he asked stone-faced, gun still aimed towards her.

"Can you put that thing away?" She requested softly. Ari hated guns, but unfortunately, she wasn't a stranger to them. She was nervous enough, fidgeting with her fingers, shifting her weight from one foot to the other.

Tommy watched her pretty eyes dart from him to her fingers, as she nervously played with them. Her pretty jet-black hair was lifted up into a sloppy bun and she had a few strings hanging in her face. Her full lips were glossy and he could sense worry in her. He was worried. He had just dropped her off a few hours ago, and they hadn't said a word to each other the entire time they were together. Things were awkward, but yet he was just happy to be in her presence. He didn't know why she was here. He knew she wasn't here to harm him, or was she? He pushed that thought from his mind, feeling guilty that he would ever let that cross it. He chalked it up to his own insecurities with her. He hadn't been around her, he hadn't protected her in months, he wasn't sure where they stood in each other's lives. She wanted him out and here she was. Tommy was bombarded with emotions that he couldn't control. He was angry with her for leaving, but he missed her. He missed her, so much that he couldn't tear his eyes away.

"My bad what's up?" he loosened up, and placed the .357 revolver on the table and made his way over to her to take the bag out of my hand, placing it on the ground with everything else that had dropped. "I had to leave." she mumbled and broke down crying again.

Ari was tired of Malik's jealous ways. She was tired of hearing about what he'd done for her and how she wasn't shit. She was starting to hate him and she was done living with an insecure man who was trying to bring her down because of his own insecurities.

"Ari" Tee said pulling her into a hug.

It had been months since she'd stepped foot in his home and had a casual conversation with Tee, but he was the same. She'd always felt safe and protected with his arms around her just like they were now. Ari was flooded with so many emotions.

"Did he put his hands on you?" Tee mumbled after taking a deep breath. He wasn't sure if he was ready to hear her answer knowing that he would probably lose it and make sure that Malik would take his last breath tonight.

"No" she replied softly, tucking her head deeper into the nape of his neck.

She cried being here with Tee, she cried because she knew she didn't have to deal anymore with what she'd been dealing with for the past few months. She sat on the end of his bed Indian style, unable to control her tears. Tee held her like always and she let it all out. How could she not?

He was her best friend. He hurts when she hurts, and vice versa. They had a connection that no one would understand. She could smell his Creed cologne, the only scent he wore, and took it all in.

"Tee I'm sor" was all she managed to push out her lips before he interjected.

"Shhhh you don't gotta say that" he whispered. "You're always welcome here."

"No, the way ..." and she was interrupted again, but this time with a kiss. Deepening the kiss, Tee laid Ari back without missing a beat. He propped himself on his elbow passionately looking into her honey eyes. He'd always loved her eyes, they were his favorite feature on her. She couldn't help but to wonder what was going through his head at the moment. Softly kissing her forehead followed by soft kisses on the nape of her neck he traced a path down to her navel. He removed her clothes ever so gently. Kissing around her Kitty Boo, he took her into his mouth devouring her juices. She let out soft moans and arched her back as the feeling of ecstasy took over. She was wet, soaking wet. So, wet she could feel it dripping down her thighs.

His only thoughts being how much he missed her, and needed to feel her. He wanted to taste her, wanting so badly to have her in every way possible. Tee needed her, all of her.

"This pussy taste so good Ari" he moaned, continuing to take his time.

That was one thing that had always been great about Tee's and Ari's sex, he was soft and gentle with her. He sucked hard and with every "mmm" he let out it made her thighs tighten around his neck, preventing him from pulling back even if he'd tried. The vibration from his words enticed her even more. He was giving her a feeling that she needed. Pulling his head back with her legs still intertwined with his arms he just looked at her pussy. He pecked it, his lips glossy, dripping with her juices and looked at it again.

"I love this pussy" he said kissing it again.

Tee started to nibble, then suck, then nibble, then lick, then suck, then lick and before Ari knew it she cried out his name in pleasure. He suckled until she released every drop into his mouth. Moving up her body slowly, he removed his pajama pants and freed his penis. It sprung up and stuck straight out at her, with a slight curve to the left. Wiping his mouth, spreading her wide as he entered her love canal.

"Ooohhhh Tee" she moaned taking in his fullness. She couldn't believe this was happening. They were friends and friends didn't make love.

"Damn Ari" he moaned into her ear. He watched her facial expressions as he stroked, thrusting inside her deep and long.

"Oh god" she moaned, already feeling another orgasm rise.

"This pussy is exactly how I remembered, cum for me Ari" Tee said continuing to stroke so deep that Ari could feel it in her soul. She wanted Tee to see the love faces she made, to hear the sounds of her agreeing and feel her feminine juices flow. She wanted him to have all of her body and didn't care that they were just friends anymore. This is Tee. *Her* Tee.

"Oh Tee" she moaned deeply.

"Cum for me baby" he said as he reached around to pinch her clit, bringing her to her highest peak and causing her to explode faster and harder than before.

"Tee" she moaned as she came, her body relaxing instantly.

He was such a softy when it came to her, making sure that she got hers first every time. You would never think he was this hard thug, one of the head generals in the most notorious drug operations internationally.

"That's it baby let it out" Tee said as he kissed her hitting his climax too. She couldn't believe what had just happened. She'd actually slept with Tee.

"Omg Tee did you strap up?" she felt the bed for any trace of the soiled rubber, realizing that he hadn't.

"No. What, you can't have my baby?" he said looking in her eyes. His question opening an old wound, bringing her to tears. "Look Ari I'm sorry" he said.

Ari put her hand up to silence him. "Don't worry" she mumbled standing, remembering those same words having been spoken some time ago.

----> More Than a Friend <----

"Living in the moment and I don't care who sees, I'm living in the moment all I need is you baby…"

Chapter 18

Tommy knew he shouldn't have said those words knowing what had happened last time he'd spoken them. He still hadn't come to any peace from that himself, after they had lost their baby, should their little girl rest in peace. Tommy had gotten her pregnant back when she was only 16. He was 18 at the time but was ready for whatever when it came to Ari. She was five months and was barely showing and they were the only ones who knew except for their close friends.

One night she called him crying and screaming. He went to her house to find she had gotten beaten badly by her father. That was the first time he'd ever heard about that, even after all the years they'd been friends prior. He had taken her to the family and told them about their situation. Tommy's dad let her stay the night with them and said that they would talk the next morning. In the middle of the night she'd had a miscarriage.

"Ari, are you okay?" Tommy worried standing on the outside of the door.

"Tee that was bad, very bad" she spoke softly and he could hear her muffled sniffles.

"Please open the door Pooch" he said wanting to make her feel better. That was a pet name that he called her normally when they were alone and he was being playful, or trying to make her feel better. When she opened the door, Tommy pulled her out and kissed her. He was relieved that she was okay despite the few tears still trickling down her face. She stared at him for a moment. He gently cupped her face in the palm of his hands and kissed her streaming tears. Tommy loved this woman and there was no denying that. His heart raced as he waited for any sign that she wasn't okay. He stared deep into her eyes and began to tell her something that he needed her to know, something that she should've already known.

"You know nothing is going to happen, and if you were to get pregnant you and that baby would have everything that you needed."

"I just don't want to be pregnant Tee."

"I know." he watched intensely as her naked body moved gracefully throughout the bedroom. She slipped into the tee shirt he had tossed across the chaise and snuggled her small body under the thick covers. He did his normal night routine, making sure they were locked in and his bitches were running loose downstairs and then he joined her. She was lying awake staring blankly at the T.V. and he wrapped his arms around her, placing his hands between her warm thighs. Tommy held her until she fell asleep.

Hearing her soft breathing, Tommy was pretty certain she was knocked out for the night, he got up and threw on a pair of black Timb's and all-black jogging suit. He called QB and headed out to pick him and Mills up. When they pulled up outside of Malik's and Ari's condo all the lights were off. He saw Danny parked and knew he was still casing. Using the key, he'd swiped from Ari, they walked straight in.

"Oh, bitch you just gon' leave, probably ran to that bitch nigga Tommy and his family" Malik barked as he walked around the corner flicking on the lights, surprised to see that it was Tommy.

"What, cat got yo tongue?" Tommy sarcastically replied.

Going straight for his face, Tommy connected with the first punch. Malik put up a little fight swinging and knocking Tommy back. He tried to get up and run back to the hallway he'd just come from, but Tommy grabbed his leg and dragged him back into the living room. This time QB came up and grabbed Malik's arms. Tommy looked up at QB irritated and he shrugged his shoulders. Tommy felt like he could handle Malik's lame ass by himself, and that he didn't need QB's assistance. Tommy did want to get in and get out so he hit him a few more times to the face and QB let him go while Mills and Danny stood back watching.

Malik didn't even try to swing after the last few punches Tommy threw, connecting with his narrow jawline. Tommy stomped him until his body went limp and he stopped moving. Tommy thought about every time he'd seen Ari with a bruise or slap mark on her face. He thought about the tears that he'd just kissed not even two hours ago; Malik closed his eyes, but Tommy had no intention of letting him off that easy. After about five minutes Malik finally got his equilibrium together and sat looking up at Tommy and his niggas. Blood was dripping from his mouth and he had knots on his head.

"So, this what you gon' do brah" Tommy said making sure he understood everything coming out of his mouth. "You gon' tell li'l mama it's over, pack her shit up tonight and have it ready when she come here tomorrow. And nigga if you even think about telling her about this li'l talk I'll put a bullet in yo fuckin head … feel me?" Tommy asked him after he was done.

"Yeah man Tommy I feel you man I'm sorry."

"Tell that to Ari and don't think I won't have someone watching outside until she leaves nigga don't try shit with her, or my nigga gon' put yo ass to sleep" Tommy stated, walking out followed by QB, Danny and Mills.

"That nigga was 'bout to kick yo ass" QB joked as the two of them hopped into Tommy's truck and Mills and Danny into Danny's.

"Nigga shut up" Tommy said as they pulled off the street. We drove to a few spots to handle some business.

Tommy had a "fuck a nigga up" attitude so nobody was safe.

When he walked into the house it was quiet. Ari was still sound asleep laying in her nighty. He figured she must have gotten up while he was gone and took a shower. She was the same old Ari as always.

*****

Ari woke up to Tee climbing into the bed kissing on her. This was so hard for her because she knew she was cheating on Malik, but she couldn't stop. Tee's love would never compare to anybody's. She loved him so much and for that she would do anything for him. They were not just friends, they were more than that. The fact that she mattered to him is all that mattered at times. She knew that as long as he was by her side she was good. She wondered if they could actually have the type of relationship where they could sleep together and act like nothing happened. She figured, this is what they had to do. She knew she wasn't one of his hoes or jump-offs, she held a special place in his heart, but she was sure that people would still call it what they wanted to.

"Ohhh Tee" she moaned as he slipped inside her wet sex.

"I'ma make you feel good okay?" he moaned as he continued to thrust softly.

"Yes Tee, make me feel good."

It wasn't long before they both climaxed and were lying in each other's arms, spent once again. She missed Tee and the family and considered possibly starting to attend the meetings and dinners again, just no late night love sessions between her and Tee. She knew that as long as she was breathing she could never *live* in a world that Tee didn't *exist* in.

----> More Than a Friend <----

"A man scorn may be worse than a female scorn"

Chapter 19

Ari woke up in Tee's arms naked. She got up, swaying into the bathroom and hopped into the shower, letting the water run through her hair and down her body. She had brought everything she needed to shower when she'd packed her bag last night. She grabbed the Design Essential shampoo and lathered up her hair. As she scrubbed, her thoughts traveled back to her and Tee. She cared strongly for Tee but knew they were better as friends. She felt what happened last night shouldn't happen again. She rinsed and grabbed the conditioner. After she felt satisfied enough she washed up with the Dove soap she'd brought. After she finished with the rest of her hygiene routine, she walked out fully dressed with her hair done. Ari knew that she looked good and she felt even better. Even with her puffy eyes from all the crying she'd done the night before.

"Damn you are really sexy Ari" Tee said eyeing her.

"Thanks Tee" she smiled looking down shyly.

"Why do you still get shy around me after all these years?" he asked walking up on her and wrapping his strong arms around her. He placed a quick kiss on her neck.

"I don't know, just do" she said. "I'ma head home and I'll call you later okay?"

"You do that. Do you want me to ride?" Tee asked searching the room for his shoes.

"Nope I'm good" she assured him before sauntering out the room. Tommy had no idea that she had no intentions on calling him later. She couldn't go down that road with him again.

Ari felt a wave of nervousness the entire ride back to the condo she shared with Malik. She wasn't ready to face him at all. She was still trying to ignore the fact he'd threatened her with a bat. If Tee would have known the details Malik probably wouldn't be standing right now. He would have been beaten or worse, six feet underground without a proper burial. When she walked into the house all her things were packed and sitting by the door. Confused she couldn't help but ask herself aloud, "What the hell was going on?"

"What is going on Malik?" she screamed through the house.

"You gotta go" he said walking around the corner looking like hell.

"What happened to you?" she asked looking at his two black eyes and swollen lips. Part of her was laughing on the inside, but then she really looked and realized he could barely open his eyes.

"I got robbed last night" he responded nonchalantly.

Ari couldn't tell if he was lying or not because he didn't form any expressions. Then again, the men who had robbed her a few months ago, had her ID and everything, so they could have come back and tried to get more things.

"Jesus Malik, you need a doctor! What else did they get?" she questioned walking over to touch him.

Moving back, he stated dryly and without emotion, "You need to leave."

"Where am I gonna go? How you gon' just put me out of our condo?" she asked on the verge of tears. She didn't have anywhere else to go and he knew that. The day they decided that she would move in with him he'd promised he would move out before he would let her be homeless.

"Just leave Ari" he said turning and walking away.

All she wanted was to be loved. All she'd ever wanted was to wake up and be happy that she was breathing, *living*. It hadn't been that way in a very long time. With his help, she moved everything out, not putting up anymore fight. It was probably for the best.

She sat in her car contemplating her next move. It was a hot mid-summer's day and a few of her white neighbors were outside spraying their lawns and tending to their gardens. It was even a family of four outside; the mother who looked as though she was pregnant again, a little blond haired girl standing at her side blowing bubbles, the father who was trimming the hedges of their trees and their other little baby was in a swing. She couldn't help but to grow sad within, wondering if she would ever have that? A family who loved her and that she equally loved back? She felt like she would never know. What she did know was that right now her boyfriend of over two years had thrown her out on her ass. She was left without a pot to piss in. She didn't have a job so getting a place would be hard. She'd never had a job so getting one of those would be hard too. She never thought she would be here. She wasn't afraid as much as she thought she would be had this ever happened. One thing she did know was that T.A.A had bred her and she was prepared and ready for whatever.

Before Ari knew it, she was back at Tee's house. She waited before going in wondering how he would react with her staying with him for a few days. He wasn't home so she put everything in the back room. She found a blanket, got comfortable on his big brown chaise and turned on the T.V. losing herself in it.

*****

Malik waited until Ari'Yonnah walked out, watching as she got into the 2009 Audi A8 he'd purchased for her a few months back. He'd actually gotten a good deal on it. A girl that he was cheating on Ari with worked at the car lot and gave him every discount she could. She must've thought it was for her or something because he was sure that if she knew it was for his woman she wouldn't have been so helpful.

    Malik loved Ari and he didn't want to see her go. He sat back flinching from his broken rib. No, he hadn't gone to the hospital, but he knew it was bruised or broken, during his years of football he'd experienced a lot. Malik lifted up a little and noticed that she was still in the driveway. He searched the block not forgetting Tommy's threat. It did take everything in him not to run out and ask her not to leave, to tell her that Tommy had done this to him and to stay with him. he couldn't though. His pride and the fact he knew Tommy would come back for him and this time he might not survive. He didn't know if she was even worth it. But he was only playing himself because she was definitely worth it and didn't deserve the things he'd been doing to her over the months. He couldn't help it though, it was in his blood. He watched until she pulled out the drive. Little did Miss Ari know her father had come by a few months back while she was in Jamaica and he'd lied to him, telling him that they were no longer together and he didn't know where she was. But it just so happened that he knew where Kyra was. Let's see how Mr. Anderson will protect his "best friend" now. Malik went to the back room and retrieved the little blue piece of paper he'd written the number on and dialed it.

    "Hello" the deep baritone voice boomed through the phone.

----> More Than a Friend <----

"Evil is as evil does"

Chapter 20

Tommy started laughing when Meka clicked the phone on him. "She got mad and hung up on me, saying I was taking up for you" he chortled looking at Mills.

Mills had come to his house around five in the morning and said they'd gotten into it, so of course Tommy let him stay the night. He could tell that his cousin was wearing thin on Mills and was almost certain that he was still with her only to keep the peace. Tommy had to admit to himself that he was partially the reason she was the way she was.

"Ari, we about to roll, you gon' be good?" he yelled out peeking into his bedroom. Damn, he thought to himself not wanting to leave. She was lying on the bed with some little shorts on and a beater with no bra.

"I'm cool, I got a showing at 4:00 for Style's shop" she responded quickly glancing back at him then refocusing back on the television.

"You know I don't want you working there" Tommy fussed. He didn't want her around a whole bunch of niggas all day, including niggas he didn't fuck with like that.

"I know Tee but I gotta work somewhere" she whined with pleading eyes, as she turned back to give him that look that only she could give. Her eyes did something to a nigga.

"Ai'ight, I'ma get somebody from my team to look after you so I know you will be" he gave in, before walking out and making a call to Style's shop.

Tommy and Mills hopped into Tommy's car after his boy at the shop said he had him for sure. Tommy knew Ari could do hair really good, but he had to let his man know he had to hire her and Tommy would drop him off a little incentive for his troubles. Style's was cool with Ari so he didn't want too much, just a few bags of "So, what exactly are you trying to do with the team?" Mills queried.

"I'm trying to straighten shit up so we can get this bread, secure a few businesses and get the show on the road!" Tommy answered merging onto the highway. He had a major plan that he'd only shared details with QB about. He needed his brother from another mother to be down with what he was talking before he felt comfortable making moves. Once QB agreed he knew it would be only a matter of time that shit was going to hit the fan. Like any other major move, most people don't be with it so they both knew they would have to sacrifice a little to gain a lot.

"Man, I think I'm done with Meka" Mills stated and Tommy looked over at him. "She just ain't been the same lately, tripping on everything" he continued as he lit a blunt, hit it and passed it to Tommy. "I ain't had no hoes come to her since we were little niggas but shorty on something different."

Tommy didn't know how comfortable he was listening to his nigga discuss his business with his little cousin. Tommy also knew he was someone Mills felt he could confide in, so Tommy told him what he would tell any other nigga.

"Have a sit down and if she ain't talking what you want to hear, do what you gotta do!"

That's the nature of the game. If you fucking with a real street nigga, he ain't going to be about no problems, no extra hoes or nothing. He going to be about his money and that's it.

Tommy walked into QB's crib and saw he was counting money with a bandage on his neck. "Shorty what happened to you?" he asked worried some lame niggas might have gotten after him. He knew his brother and that that wasn't the case because Tommy would've been on speed dial had it been.

"Man, my lady sliced me up the other day after she beat my side bitch up!" he replied shaking his head, obviously thinking about it all over again.

"Man, y'all niggas better grow up and stop fuckin' 'round with hoes that want drama!" Tommy shot knowledge to them both. He took a drag off the blunt QB handed him and felt lightheaded. He was high as fuck and thought he heard moving in the back.

"Who here with you?" Tommy asked.

"Nobody" he answered looking behind us too. "Nigga you high, calm the fuck down!"

"Like I was saying, this, two bitches at the same time gotta come to an end sooner or later. Find you one bad loyal ass bitch and make her wifey!" Tommy waved off the blunt that had made its way back to him too fast. "Life will be much easier, especially at the meetings."

The three of them conversed a little more and then made their way out. Tommy had to talk to QB about some shit he wasn't sure he could trust Mills with, so he decided to wait to holler at him later. Heading his own way in one of QB's cars, he glanced down as his phone started to ring and he noticed it was Kyra.

"Danny? You home?" Kyra called out searching the house. He was nowhere to be found. She figured he must be out working. She walked upstairs where he had a few bags scattered on the bed; Juicy Couture, Prada, Macys, Forever 21, and Footlocker. "Aww baby" she smiled, knowing he'd gone shopping for her. She was so happy and loved when he did things like this. Kyra and Danny had been together since she was 16, ever since Ari moved out of her father's house and in with Tommy's family. She would go over Tommy's and spend time with Ari days at a time and with that came Tommy's friends. Yes, they were two and three years older than the girls, but that didn't steer their interest away. They all had an impenetrable bond like no other, most people wouldn't understand. Smiling just thinking about how much she was in love with Danny, she knew for sure he was out working because all of this had to cost a lot.

Kyra took time and hung the clothes up before she started on dinner. She knew she had to meet Ari at four since she was going to be her model for her showing with Style's. Kyra was prepared to be super fly for her best friend. She knew she was a cold hairstylist and would go far. She'd been doing my hair for as long as Kyra could remember. Her best friend was very creative all the way around from hair styles, drawing and design, even decorating.

"I'll be to get you at 3:30" Kyra told Ari when she returned her call. Kyra knew she was nervous because this was her fourth time calling her today, making sure she was going to be on time and that she didn't mess what she had done to her hair up already.

Kyra put the rest of her food into the slow-cooker and pulled her leather jacket from the closet. She opened the door to walk out and saw a face that she never wanted to see.

"Kyra, where is she?" Ari'Yonnah's father stood looking down at me. "Where is my daughter" he asked her again as she stood there speechless.

Kyra hated this bastard and wished Danny was here because she would've had him put a bullet between this bastard's eyes. She remembered the first time she saw him hurt her best friend.

"Thank you so much sis, I needed this done so much" I said hugging Ari as she stood looking at her hard work.

"If it wasn't for my mama I wouldn't know anything about hair

girl" she said. "You talked to Tommy today?" I asked her knowing most likely she had.

"Girl you know we talk every day" she said and then paused.

"What? Un uh what you gotta tell me?" I said turning to her, seeing that she had started to turn red.

"Kyra" she started smiling "we ya know ..."

Taking a minute, I blurted out "Y'all had sex?" I asked her excitedly since she was the only virgin left.

Shaking her head, she responded, "Yeah." "Omg I'm so happy for ..." was all I was able to get out when the door swung open. "OH! SO, YOU'RE HAVING SEX NOW?" her daddy screamed as he charged her. I stood frozen as he cocked back with her head in one hand forcing it to collide with his fist. The only thing I could do was stand paralyzed from fear and screaming, telling him to stop. He picked me up and literally carried me out the house as I stood crying and listening to her screams. I couldn't see her for a whole month after that.

Kyra snapped out of her trance as he still stood towering over me asking again, "Kyra, where is she? Where is my daughter?"

*****

"Yo" Tommy looked at his phone recognizing the voice on the other end right off the bat. Tommy was headed to holler at the uncles about what he'd heard the other day.

"Tommy, we need to meet now" Kyra said in the phone sounding as if she was driving.

"Where you at?" Tommy asked alarmed by her eagerness.

"Tommy, he's back and he's looking for her" Kyra said now sounding like she was crying.

"Who's back?" Tommy asked confused.

"Ari's daddy!" she cried.

"Where's Ari?" Tommy questioned.

"I'm picking her up now" Kyra responded.

"Okay Kyra I'ma need you to muster up a cool face ai'ight. Don't let her know anything is up."

"But Tommy she needs to know!"

"NO!" he yelled not meaning to. "Don't tell her Ky" he said knowing how little mama would react if she knew he was looking for her again.

"Okay" she said sounding a little calmer.

"I'm sorry Kyra but she doesn't need this on her right now" Tommy couldn't help but to think about how he didn't either. Hanging up, he was a little relieved that Ari's father didn't know where she was because if he did he would've gone straight to her.

When Tommy reached Uncle Tevin's house he was sitting on the porch by himself. He walked up and dapped him up before taking a seat. "You look stressed son. What's going on?" he asked while sipping a Corona.

Wasting no time, Tommy got straight to business. "I am Unc. For starters, Ari's pops done popped back up" he said looking at him.

"I hate that sick fucking bastard," he said and Tommy knew he was telling the truth because he frowned and took a deep breath. "Unfortunately, son we knew this day would come."

Tommy's uncles and pops were some emotional ass men and let their feelings take over them more often than not. They couldn't control their tempers. It was good they held the positions they had because they would have been in jail years ago, he thought to himself.

"I also wanted to talk to y'all because I heard some shit that's been weighing on me heavy." Tommy paused and Uncle Tevin looked into his eyes. He didn't know how to go about what he'd heard them talk about a couple of weeks ago, but then again it was better than not knowing.

"Do I gotta sister?"

----> More Than a Friend <----

"I'll Ride for you; Baby I'll die for you"

Chapter 21

Ari jumped into the front seat of Kyra's silver Jeep Cherokee, her leather seats cool even though the sun was blazing through the window. Looking over at her, Ari placed her black Louis Vuitton shades on her face to shield her eyes from the bright sun.

"What's wrong?" Ari inquired. Kyra looked as if she had been crying or shaken up by something. She was Ari's number one and if she was feeling some kind of way Ari was going to see what she could do to change that.

"Girl what you talking 'bout?" Kyra said, trying to mask whatever had her feeling the way she was feeling.

"So, we're keeping secrets? Something is up" Ari said fixing a couple pieces of Kyra's hair.

"I'm good girl, you know if something was up I would let you know!" she replied keeping the lie going.

Ari side-eyed her trying to read her, but left it alone.

"Why Meka call today tripping on me?" Ari said knowing she was going to have something to say. It was true, Meka had called Tee's cell earlier looking for Mills and Ari answered it. Ari figured Meka didn't know that she was staying there but it wasn't any of her business either.

"Whatever, that girl is just jealous of you honey don't worry about it."

"I don't know what it is but she supposed to be my sis."

"Girl you should already know you can't trust any females but me, because you know I'd die for you."

Knowing Kyra was serious Ari responded with "I'd die for you too" as she looked out the window and prayed that neither one of them would ever have to.

Ari walked into Style's and it was a lot of people, either waiting to be serviced or being serviced. The shop was big in size and had top of the line sinks and dryers. He checked out Kyra's hair and said he liked it. He also let Ari know that they were like family and that of course she had a place in his shop. She was too happy, now she could get herself together.

Kyra dropped Ari back off after the showing. Seeing Tee sitting in his boxers Ari walked in and jumped on his lap.

"Guess what bestie, I got the job!" she said excited.

"That's what's up" he said looking at the television. He seemed distracted and he was a little drunk too, Ari could smell the liquor on his breath.

"Look let me tell you" Ari said cupping his face, trying to get him to focus on her.

"I'm listening go head" he said steady looking past her.

"Ugh forget it" she said storming up the stairs.

She climbed into the shower and washed her body as she thought about the shoes she would wear tonight to the meeting. The doors swung open and she was pulled out and carried into the bedroom. Instead of throwing her on the bed, Tommy lifted her up onto his shoulders and began to devour her. Ari, moaning like crazy was trying not to fall off his shoulders. Tommy was a small dude but he was very strong. He walked over to the wall still holding her in the air without missing a beat.

"OMG Tommy" she moaned loud and her mind started to race. When he finished pleasing her orally, he slid her down right onto his hard dick with one swift movement.

"Ahhhhh oohhhh Tee!" she shrieked not even realizing he had stripped out of his bottoms. He started stroking her deep and long, but forceful on the wall.

"You forgive me" he asked thrusting while he awaited a reply.

"Yes! I forgive you just please don't stop" she moaned creeping up on her orgasm.

"You like it like this?" he asked slowing down.

"Yes Toommmmmyyyyyy, don't stop."

"Do you love me?" he asked steady stroking.

"I love you Tee" she said not wanting him to stop.

"No.... are you IN love me with me" he asked steady stroking, but slowing down even more.

"Mmmmm Tee don't stop" she begged thrusting her hips hard, forcing his shaft to dig deeper into her love canal.

"ANSWER ME ARE.... YOU....IN...LOVE.... WITH....ME?" he asked, giving hard and deep long strokes.

"Oh! Tee I'm coming!" she said releasing and falling limp as he held her, but still thrusting so he could get his.

"Damn" he said as he released. "I love you Ari."

"I love you too Tee" she replied. She just wasn't sure if she was *in* love with him.

*****

Tommy sat on the edge of the bed sipping on some Henny while he waited for Ari to finish the last touches to her hair. She was so beautiful and always kept herself up. It hurt him bad that she wouldn't say she was in love with him, but he couldn't force her to do anything.

"You done yet?" he asked watching her put on her post diamond earrings.

"Yeah" she said walking a little funny. "Are you cool?" he asked her wondering if she was going to be able to stick out the meeting. Tommy was happy she was going back with him again, it had been hard without her. He smiled taking in her fit for the night. She was dressed in an olive green Pink sweat-suit and her ass was bulging out so far you could sit a cup on it. Her hair was pulled up into a curly ponytail and at first glance she looked as if she was going running. She had a pair of Gucci Jordan's on her feet that matched his.

"Yeah you kinda made me a li'l swollen" she said wincing.

"I'm sorry" Tommy apologized. He knew he'd put it on her, but his ego boosted 3-times as he thought; 'that's what I do'. Looking at his ringing phone, he walked into the hall to answer it, "Yo".

"Tommy." he knew exactly who it was already.

"What's good Davina?" he asked her wondering why the hell she was calling him. Tommy left her and JaMila's ass alone as soon as Ari had moved in. He didn't want her and he knew she was in her feelings, but she had to know she would never be his bitch.

"Why you doing me like this Tommy? You just gon move that bitch back in? She doesn't even love you Tommy" she whined. "Meka told me …" was all she got out before he interrupted her.

"I ain't fuckin' wit ya shorty, stop calling my fuckin phone" he said before clicking on her. He made a mental note to check Meka's ass about telling bitches in the street family business. He didn't want to be with Davina anyway because she was really a hoe. JaMila on the other hand was a good girl, but he needed Ari and only Ari. He needed all of his attention on her and his work. Tommy wanted Ari to trust him, so he could get her back in love with him. He had been trying to knock her up for the past month and a ½ since she moved back in with him. He wanted a family and he wanted that with Ari.

"Who was that?" Ari asked walking up on him.

"Nobody, you ready?"

"Yeah."

Tommy and Ari jumped in the car and strapped up. Tommy pulled into traffic and decided to make a quick stop at the gas station. He hopped out and went in when he bumped into his nigga Wayne who he hadn't seen in a while, not since high school. Shorty did a twelve-year bid because he and his boys robbed a burger spot when they were young and he wouldn't give them up. Wayne took that seven strong and three months after he went down, both his boys got popped trying to rob a pizza shop.

"What's good my nigga, let me holler at you!" he asked and Tommy followed him out. Tommy didn't think he was on no trash so he felt comfortable following. He glanced over at Ari who was talking on her phone and looking in the other direction.

Wayne had every intention to rob the gas station he had been watching for three days. It had been a hard time for him lately, trying to maintain. He took a deep breath and prayed to God to give him a break. He wanted to make enough money off this, so he could use the money to get his life stable. He said another silent prayer as he reached into the pocket of his hoodie to retrieve the .357 revolver just when he heard the ding of the door and in walked someone he hadn't seen in years. Tommy Anderson.

Tommy Anderson was someone he went to middle school with and they were cool. Wayne instantly looked to the ceiling thanking God. He was the answer to the prayer he had just sent to heaven not 5 seconds before. Wayne knew Tommy was born into money and from the look of the car he rolled up in he still was getting it. Tommy may be the one to put Wayne in a better position. Humbling himself he asked if they could walk outside to talk.

"What you doing here my nigga, I heard you moved uptown out the way" Tommy said freaking the mild he had just bought.

"I did" he said and did a quick look around the parking lot.

"What you doing here?"

Wayne looked back at the store and then Tommy realized he was either casing the joint or he was about to rob that bitch just when he walked in. tommy had to respect it though, at least he was hitting businesses and not a nigga like him.

"Listen bruh I'ma toss you my number and I want you to make a trip back down here and meet up with me.

I'ma look out for you my nigga, word ai'ight, let this shit go son" Tommy said and meant every word. Tommy reached in his pocket and pulled out ten one hundred dollar bills and handed them over. Nigga was a grinder and he could secure another joint since Wayne lived up in New York. Thanking Tommy, they dapped on it and Tommy jogged back to the car.

"*Finally*, Damn nigga," Ari barked irritated and he laughed and continued to their destination.

----> More Than a Friend <----

"Life's Lemons"

Chapter 22

Anthony waited patiently as Kyra pulled into traffic. He knew sooner or later she would lead him to his daughter. He cracked his neck, looking into the rearview mirror before pulling out after her. He hoped Ari didn't think her little thug ass boyfriend and his family could keep him away from her forever. He wanted to get rid of her once and for all. Ever since the day his wife had brought her home she'd been a problem for them. He never wanted the little bitch anyway. He wanted it to be his wife and him forever, just the two of them! It wouldn't have mattered if Ari was his biological daughter or not.

The Lord had made sure at an early age that Anthony would never be able to have kids when he made the doctor cut his nuts on accident. At least that's what they called it when his mother sued and they apologized before settling out of court. Anthony's wife wanted Ari but he never did because he felt it wasn't in God's plan. Anthony had been punished and that's why GOD took his loving wife from him and reminded him every day, every time he looked at *her*. GOD reminded Anthony that invitro was ungodly and by having done it they'd been cursed.

He slammed on the brakes as soon as he'd laid eyes on her. She looked so much like Mary that he couldn't help but miss her even more. Ari also looked just like that asshole brother of his too. He hated him and he hated *her* even more.

"Excuse me sir you can't park here," a blond overweight lady said as she tapped lightly on his window. Instead of responding he just pulled off. He now knew where they liked to hang out and that was enough for him. He had followed Kyra here for two weeks since he showed up at her door. He figured either she worked there or she got her hair done here.

----> More Than a Friend <----

"Blast from the past"

Chapter 23

After the meeting the other night, Tommy had finally gotten the whole story from his old man. It weighed heavy on him for so many different reasons. He pulled the covers back and wrapped his arms around Ari.

"My father cheated on my mother with one of her best friends and she had a baby," he blurted out. Ari jumped up, turning to look into his eyes.

"What?!" She covered her mouth like she couldn't believe what she'd just heard.

He continued, needing to get it off his chest. Tommy couldn't trust anyone else with this information like he knew he could trust her. His father had basically threatened him to keep his secret. His father is reckless and Tommy wasn't trying to test his gangsta. Besides, he still didn't know what he even thought, or wanted to do with this info.

"I guess the chick moved away and cut all ties with him and when she came back she was pregnant." Ari was quietly listening so he kept going. "I guess being the man my pops' was he wanted to take the baby from her, but she wouldn't give her up. As fucked up as it sounds my dad decided he didn't want anything to do with her since she wouldn't let him take the baby. I guess she fell in love with her doctor and he helped raise the baby. When pops reached out again he was rejected so he decided to never contact her or have anything to do with her or the little girl anymore." he'd finally gotten it all out. Ari shifted and softly placed her hand on his chest.

"Does mama know? They kept this from you all your life?"

"Ma don't know about the baby, but she did know that the lady and my dad was fuckin' though. I guess they were best friends, her and QB's mom and my mom's." He couldn't believe none of this himself. He had a sister out there a few months younger than himself and they didn't even know each other.

"Uncle Tevin gave her mom's some money every month and even started a fund for the little girl to go to college or something, but he said her mom was killed and they hadn't heard anything since." Tommy felt for the girl wherever she was, she had no one and that would be hard for anybody.

"Damn that's fucked up" Ari still had a look of misbelief on her face.

Tommy still couldn't believe it himself. He felt like he wanted to find her and build a relationship or something. They were grown, so you couldn't really know for sure the type of person she had become. She might not even know she has family out here, or that she was adopted.

Tommy took a deep breath and Ari gave him a peck on his forehead. She didn't stop there, her soft lips kissed his nose, lips and then chest hairs. She stopped and looked at him. She was always so modest and never was the first one to start up the love sessions, but he could tell from the look she gave him she wanted some of daddy.

"Tell me you want this dick," Tommy whispered and pinched her pussy while she seductively stared into his eyes. Her body jerked and her back arched so deep it made her body semi-lift off the bed. "Damn Ari it's like that?" he grinned. He knew from her reaction that she was yearning for what was soon to come. When he had sex with Ari it was more than fucking. Even when it was hard it was more love-making than anything. He wanted to always please her before he got his. Tommy rolled on top of her and kissed her lips. She looked into his eyes just watching him.

"What you want me to do?" Tommy asked and she smiled covering her face. "Tell me."

"Kiss her" she said without taking her hands down. He smiled at how childish she was being.

"Only if you watch me."

Tommy repositioned himself down between her legs. Getting comfortable, he pulled her panties off. As soon as he kissed her pussy she groaned and tore her hands from her face. He put his whole face in her sweet spot and inhaled. He loved her scent. He licked her clit and started to go in, licking and sucking. She moaned, and started to lift her hips pushing her pussy into his mouth.

"Mmmmm Ari you taste so good" he moaned and she grabbed his head. He looked up and saw her watching him with hungry eyes, mouth open wide.

"Tee, you ..." he interrupted her train of thought when he sucked hard and her body shook violently.

Tommy felt a gush of wetness rush into his mouth and slide down his throat. He licked softer trying to get every drop she had released. Ari breathed heavily and had a few after-shock jerks before her body finally relaxed. Tommy wiped his mouth off and came up. She grabbed for his manhood and guided it into her wetness. Her touch alone had him ready to come, but that wasn't about to happen. He had so much more in store for her.

*****

Ari jolted from her dream, rose from the bed with an eerie feeling. She looked over at Tee who was still fast asleep. She stood and walked into the kitchen with her cell phone in hand. She heard the dogs in the back barking, so she went to the glass window and looked out. It was dark and she couldn't see anything. Usually Tee would let them roam freely at night so she wondered why he'd left them outside. Ari looked down and her cell phone read 3:08 a.m. She was about to open the door and let them in because they were going nuts, and started to jump on the glass doors, when she felt a hand over her mouth and was lifted into the air. She instantly started to kick and swing, but stopped when she saw that it was Tee. He motioned for her to be quiet and pointed towards the living room. Ari heard someone whispering and finally figured what was going on.

"Follow me baby" Tee he mouthed to her as he went to slide the doors open. He did a small whistle and before Ari knew it Massive and Cadence, his two pits, came running full speed into the house. We heard two different voices scream "Oh Shit!" and a bunch of rumbling.

"Stay out here" Tee ordered. Pushing Ari through the door as he ran into the room where the commotion was. Her hands were shaking and she looked down at her cell and dialed Uncle Tevin.

"Hey Ari, what's up?" he answered groggily.

"Uncle Tevin" she tried to whisper. "There is someone in the house. I'm so scared! Tee went back in with the dogs and he pushed me outside."

"Okay Ari I'm on my way" he said and she heard what sounded like him getting up and out the bed.

She didn't want to call the police, but she felt like she needed to call someone and who better than Uncle Tevin. Ari hung up and slid the door open. She didn't hear anything at all and when she turned the corner she saw everything flipped over. Tee wasn't in the room and the front door was open. She ran to the door and saw him standing with his pistol in his hand holding his head. Blood was gushing between his fingers and she panicked.

"What happened? Who was it?" She questioned, not giving him a chance to respond. Ari rushed over to him and moved his hand to see the damage.

"Man, some corny ass niggas!" Tommy was pissed and stormed into the house with her on his heels. "Go pack us a bag we getting a room!" he snapped and she froze in place. He had never used that tone with her and it had shaken her up more than she already was. Deep inside she felt that something just wasn't right. Tee had never spoken to her aggressively as he had just done.

"Tee!" she screamed and he turned fast on his heels. He must have felt where she was coming from because he pulled her into him and wrapped his arms around her. Ari was shaking she could have been killed or hurt and she didn't know what was going on. He felt bad for yelling at her like that he just needed her to do what he had asked. He wanted to get her out of there as fast as he could for that simple reason, her protection.

"Just do what I asked."

"I called Uncle Tevin he is probably on his way," she informed him. "I think you need stitches."

"I'm good, just go" he asked less forcibly than before.

Ari walked away and did exactly what he'd asked, packing a bag for both of them. She didn't want this life anymore. She could see a blast from her past all over again.

I couldn't believe that my dad had actually let the uncles and Tommy move me out with no problems, or so I was told. They informed me of this because the truth was I hadn't seen my father in a few days. They had the paperwork that said Tee's mom had taken guardianship though. I sat back in the car with Tee who'd been acting weird all day. He was focused on work, but wouldn't let me out of his sight either. At the house, everyone was whispering and tip-toeing around and I had no idea what was wrong.

"Tommy I'm really tired and just want to go home," I said yawning. It had only been a week since my miscarriage and I wasn't feeling real social. A lot had happened in the last week and I had never felt so alone. At least not since my mother had passed away some time ago.

"I ain't really feelin' leaving you alone shorty," he said. "You been real mopey and shit I don't want you to do something crazy."

"Boy take my ass to mama's I'm tired now," I said and closed my eyes.

The last thing I heard was him say "one more stop" and then I woke up to him opening my car door. He told me he had one more run and he would be back. I was happy to finally be alone. I didn't know if I could take the constant people around, in and out. It was either his friends or Mama's friends but there was never just us. I walked in and it was dark. When I made it to the stairs I heard voices in the kitchen.

"Mama" I called out and headed in that direction. Now I know he'd just said she was gone. I flicked on the light and there stood two guys in masks with their guns pointed at me.

"Where the money?" they asked.

I was frozen where I stood and didn't know what to do. I'd never seen a gun and I damn sure had never had one pointed at me. I felt a warm substance running down my legs and I knew then I had pissed on myself.

One of the men tried to rush me and just as I turned to run I was snatched back by my hair. I heard two pops and I ended up face down on the ground. I was dragged out the house and tossed into Tee's truck. Tee turned and ran back into the house and I sat embarrassed, frightened and pissy. I was not ready for this.

Yes, Ari felt safe when she was with Tee, but was she ready to be looking over her shoulder every day and every night? She made it downstairs and Uncle Tevin and Dr. Greene were standing over Tee. She'd just finished stitching him up.

"You got our stuff together?" Tee asked her. She shook her head and watched him.

"You're going to have to drive young lady" Dr. Greene informed her, walking over and giving her a soft, motherly hug. She was a family physician and an OB/GYN so she was certified. She was a family friend and had been around a long time. Ari had heard rumors that she and Uncle Tevin had had a fling back in the day and he'd even put her through school. They were rumors though, so who knew.

"Okay" Ari said and Tee walked them to the door.

"Bright and early" Uncle Tevin said and looked at Ari with a concerned look. She didn't know if it was because of what happened or something else, but she wasn't feeling too comfortable. Something was up and she wanted to know what it was. Being realistic, she knew that anytime something was going on the last person to ever find out was her. She sometimes had to ask Kyra to fill her in, and it upset her. She didn't know if they thought she couldn't handle it or what. Either way she was growing very irritated with the way they treated her as if she was still that naïve little 12-year old girl.

----> More Than a Friend <----

"Life's Cycle"

Chapter 24

Niggas couldn't just live and be cool. They had to act up and for that reason now Tommy would have to put in work to set shit straight. He looked over at Ari who had finally fallen asleep. She had her mouth and her legs wide open. He couldn't help but chuckle to himself. She had no idea what he would do for her. He wanted the two of them to be together, and be a family, but she was stuck on this friend shit. He'd take that though if it kept her close, close so he could protect her like he felt he was supposed to. He would never let her go, *never* again.

Tommy stepped into the living room of the suite they'd be staying in until he had time to secure another crib. He could hardly sleep, or even think about sleeping. He didn't know how Malik and her pops found out where he stayed, but they had him fucked up. The only thing that saved their lives tonight was Ari. He couldn't kill her father and that punk ass nigga in his house in front of her. He didn't think she would've healed from that so he let them go. But they were far from being in the clear.

"What up son?" Tommy answered his phone as he blazed a blunt.

"I got that info you need, we can do breakfast ai'ight?" his man Brown said through the phone. He was the main hitman in his camp and Tommy went to him for shit that he'd rather stay away from. Let's be real, every thug knows he can't do some shit himself. Tommy knew he was too close and personal with them lames and that he'd be the first one the DA went searching for when those niggas got popped. He planned to be in a very crowded area when that took place.

"Word" Tommy clicked and put out his blunt. He put the extra latch on the door and walked into the bedroom. He climbed right up between her legs and started to smell her sweetness. She groaned and mumbled something but never opened her eyes. He pushed her panties to the side and started placing soft kisses on her mound. Tommy loved her pussy. This time when he looked up her eyes were on him, but she looked frustrated.

"I don't give a fuck, this my pussy!" he said pushing her legs farther apart and going to work. Tommy licked and sucked on her sweetness until she gave in moaning and squirming. She rubbed his head as he feasted. He pulled back looking at her glossy clit and admired his work. She was wet and ready. Tommy slipped two fingers inside her slit and watched her eyes as she moaned and thrust her hips forward, forcing his fingers as deep as they would go. She patted her vagina while hungrily gazing into his eyes and that turned him on even more. He grabbed his dick and started stroking, watching and waiting for the perfect time to enter her. She tightened her walls around his fingers and he pulled them out replacing them with his dick. He stroked her, pushing himself deep up in her ocean, her gushy wetness sounding off. Her screams grew with each thrust, each stroke. He felt her climax spurt all over his long member and he knew she was spent. She smiled at him.

"Tee" she whined restless and her eyes closing.

"Nope I ain't done yet." Tommy tapped her legs and she rolled over and lifted her leg. "I'ma blow this pussy out tonight baby." he kissed her and sucked her neck listening to her call out his name.

"Fuck ma!" he let his load off deep up in her and passed out himself. It was hours later when he heard Ari calling his name.

"Tee wake up!"

He slowly opened his eyes. The sun was blazing through the blinds and he had to squint to keep them from burning. She was standing with her hand on her hip, fully dressed.

"How long you gon' sleep?"

Tommy didn't answer her, just frowned. 'Why did she wake me the fuck up anyway?' he thought, rolling over and grabbing his phone and saw it read 2:37 P.M. across the screen.

"Fuck!" he said rising.

"Your phone has been ringing all morning and I'm hungry!" she flopped on the bed wincing.

She grabbed at her kitty and tugged on it. He smiled knowing he put that work in and it had her feeling some type of way. Her pussy had been super tight, hot and wet lately and he loved every bit of it. He knew she just missed him more than she let on. He'd been wanting to fuck her for a while and got pissed whenever he thought about that lame Malik hitting it.

"Man, be quiet" he checked her, pulling on her trying to get her back in bed with him. She wasn't feeling it though.

"Come on Tee!" she fussed and got up, storming out the room.

Tommy got himself straight, showered and walked out fully dressed. He had on a black pair of True Religion jeans, a black tee shirt and his wheat Timb's. He walked out to find Ari asleep on the couch.

"How you fussing and back sleep?"

"Shut up, I'm really hungry!" she sat up and they walked out. Tommy fed her and dropped her off at Uncle Tevin's with Kyra and the other girls and then called Brown.

"Let's ride" he said rolling up waiting for him to come out.

*****

Ari laughed with the girls when as she looked at her phone. The last week or so she'd been getting these weird phone calls from a blocked number. You could never know who it is. She was thinking more along the lines that one of Tee's little girlfriends had gotten a hold of her number and it pissed her off. Or it could have been Malik, she hadn't talked to him since she moved out and it has been a few months. She voiced this and the girls started their man bashing.

"I wouldn't doubt it, same nigga different tricks" Juicy said patting her weave. "I wouldn't doubt if all them niggas was cheating out there together."

"As long as my bills paid" Mia added.

"Fuck that y'all hoes sound stupid!" Meka interjected and scratched her nose. "Let me find out my nigga cheating I'm going straight for them balls!"

"I must agree, I ain't dealing with that" Ari said and her phone rang again. Meka snatched it from her hands and screamed hello into the phone.

"You a sick bitch sitting here just listening! If you 'bout that life or want them problems blow down bitch!" Ari shook her head and laughed.

Meka was crazy as hell as always. It had been a minute really, since she'd moved in with Tee and since she'd seen her. Ari had been keeping her distance because she had been acting really funny lately. The girls hadn't had dinner together in months, and Ari didn't know what it was but she hadn't forgotten the way Meka acted out trying to fight her either. Kyra peeped game of course but the other girls were clueless. It was like that though, Kyra was Ari's main one so she knew her just as well as Kyra knew herself.

"Girl you don't know who that is? What if they come to kill us?" Mia stated.

"Shut yo scary ass up!" Meka shot her a mean look and she shut up.

"*Anyway*, I don't know who it is, but I'ma address it very soon because I don't want this all over again" she said referring to problems she'd had in the past with Tee and his cheating. That nigga was friendly with hoes, and because he had that pack it didn't make it any better. That nigga had been rich since she'd known him, and for that reason these dumb ass girls fell at his feet and allowed him to walk on them. Not Ari! She'd never been that type nor did she have plans on being that type. Her mind drifting because of a little secret she had been keeping for the past couple weeks.

"Please don't be on that again! Our family just got back together and the last thing we need is for y'all to fall apart!" Meka said.

Ari couldn't help but think to herself, "back together?" She didn't know about all that. Hell, little did Meka know her man was planning on leaving her ass real soon from what she'd heard.

"No, we are not back together Meka! I am just staying with him until I can find a place."

"Girl y'all are back together I don't care what you say!" Meka said and rolled her eyes. "You are in denial as always!"

"UGH!" Ari said and rolled her eyes back at her. She wasn't in denial. She didn't want any parts of him anymore. He had hurt her too bad in the past. They were better as friends and that's how she wanted them to stay. Well, with benefits that is and who's to say what they were going to be with the secret she was hiding that she had every intention of taking care of before anyone found out. Ari had a lot on her plate, and she didn't know exactly what she wanted to do. Besides bitch, worry about your nigga and why he been staying with us lately, she thought.

"See that smile?" Mia said and Ari noticed all eyes were on her.

Little did any of them know, even Kyra, she'd been stacking money and was planning to get her own spot in a few weeks, especially after what had happened last night. She wasn't trying to make anybody's headlines, *"Twenty-one-year-old woman found dead, floating in the river around 6:00 am by two fishermen who were out early for the Bass!"* Not Ari, she was going to do what she always had done. She needed to have her own and she would never make the mistake of living with another man who could put her out whenever he decided to, *especially* now.

Ari looked up and Kyra was watching her. Something just didn't seem right with her girl, it was like she had a lot on her mind, Ari thought.

"Like I said, we just friends." She couldn't stress it enough because they kept giving her funny glares. She was cool with how things were but that didn't mean she would just jump back into something with him. She and Malik had been broken up a few short months. She was still having withdrawals about him.

*****

"We were so close!" the older, but not so wiser man stated. He was so close but so far away from getting the girl he wanted. He tossed his notes to the side upset because he had planned it out perfectly until those dogs had broken through and tried to bite a hole through his legs.

"I have another plan" he said grabbing his keys walking out.

He had gotten used to sitting and watching. He sat and waited for her to walk out. It was so hard for him to catch them alone because they always stayed in groups. He called her phone and watched as she walked to her car. She answered and he breathed into the phone. Shaking her head, she looked around before jumping into her Jeep. She slowly pulled into traffic and he followed closely behind. He had to leave the football player behind because he didn't have it in him. He was a bitch. He wasn't tough and didn't have any backbone. It was better to do this without him. The man already knew he would have to eventually get rid of that loose end.

She quickly pulled into a driveway and got out the truck. It wasn't her driveway and he knew that because he'd visited her previously.

He waited until she came back out hours later. She seemed nervous, almost like she knew he was watching. She stopped and looked around before getting into her Jeep and pulled off. He had no worries, knowing he'd parked far enough that she couldn't see him. Following her again, he watched as she pulled into her driveway, after a short ten-minute drive. He knew it was now or never.

Jumping out he approached her fast, too fast for her to see him coming. He tossed the knapsack over her head and picked her up. His smile so big across his face he couldn't control himself. He cracked his neck knowing he had accomplished something.

----> More Than a Friend <----

"Cold. Colder. Coldest"

Chapter 25

  The search for Ari's father had gone cold. Malik no longer lived in the condo they'd once shared so he was gone too. Tommy had found out that he'd been released from his football team so he couldn't stake that out either. He wasn't feeling too good about this and wanted so badly to just tell Ari what was going on. He couldn't let her live with fear. The fear of not knowing exactly what her father wanted from her, or why he'd wanted it so badly. Tommy did decide that he wanted to maybe put security with her at all times. It would be better for him and her to know she had backup if needed.

  Tommy went to Uncle Tevin's and saw that the girls were all gone. He felt this was the best time to talk to Meka, who was chilling in the dining room talking to Uncle Tevin, about the things that had been going on with her. His cousin hadn't been herself, not even with him.

  "What's up?" he asked her when Uncle Tevin left out the dining room.

  "What you mean?" she answered with attitude.

  "I mean why have you been siding with bitches on the street with family business?" he quizzed. "Davina told me that you been telling her things you shouldn't even speak!"

She just looked at him with a look of what almost felt like hate. She was quiet like she was thinking long and hard about what she wanted to say. He could tell she was definitely feeling some type of way and he didn't know why. He had always treated her like the sister he'd never had. She laughed, looked at him and still didn't say anything.

"Meka what is going on with you?" he asked concerned.

"Meka what is up with you?" she mocked and pushed the food she had been eating away. "Meka what's been up with you?" she repeated. She stood up and had a look like she was high. For the first time, he noticed she was definitely high on something.

"Fuck you *Thomas*!" she said with emphasis on the "s" sound and rolled her eyes. "I'm so tired of you putting everyone above family! You be letting Mills stay with you and you supposed to be my cousin! You got that bitch Ari living with you and you so stuck up her mutha-fucking ass you don't see that she's using you! *You are so far up that bitch ass you don't see what is in front of you!*" she screamed loudly and caused Uncle Tevin to come around the corner.

"What is in front of me Meka? Are you high?" Tommy asked.

"High ass a mutha-fuckin kite!" **She laughed.**

"On what Meka?" Uncle Tevin's baritone voice asked, causing her to flinch as she just noticed his presence.

"Oh, you gon' call Uncle on me?" she asked me. "Well I'm grown and I can do what I want to do!" she said and started to do a little dance. "I can shoot if I want to shoot!" she sang and danced.

Tommy instantly became furious. He knew that nigga Mills wasn't stupid enough to have left no stash of boy at his house! He was even more fucked up because he knew what those drugs did to a person. He could tell that if his cousin had indeed gotten into some heroine it would be a long journey to get her back, if she ever came back. She was still dancing as he and Uncle Tevin exchanged looks, knowing what each other was thinking.

"I can get high if I want to" she said bending over in front of Tommy and hiking her dress up. "Twerk! Twerk! Twerk!"

Tommy pushed her off him hard, causing her to crash face forward to the ground and stormed out. He had one direction. He was going to kill Mills if he had let his cousin get into his shit!

Tommy turned off 55th and onto Lexington drive. He walked into the spot and there sat QB, Mills, Cameo and Chris. It was a little apartment that they used from time to time to meet up. It only housed a few items of furniture and nothing else. The kitchen was completely empty. The floor was carpeted but it was dark grey in color from not being properly managed.

"Please tell me you ain't leave no shit at the crib son!" Tommy asked walking in without any hi's, hello's, what up my niggas or nothing. He was on a mission to see if the dumb ass nigga had left some boy at the house and Meka had gotten into it. He walked up and Mills jumped up quick causing all the men in the room to rise.

"What you talkin' bout?" he asked seeming clueless.

Tommy knew then that nigga knew exactly what he was speaking on and he knew that's why Mills had wanted to leave her. Why he didn't he tell him about his fam though? He felt more betrayed than anything. The right thing to do would be to come to him and explain what was going on. Not have him out here looking dumb like he didn't know what was going on in his set. He felt Mills betrayed his cousin because he had not even tried to help her, he was just going to leave her. Everything made sense now, her actions over the past couple of months and her disloyalty to the fam. Tommy was fucked up off this one.

He upped the strap and put it to Mills head and he threw his hands up and sat back onto the Lazy Boy he was sitting on.

"Bitch nigga you know what I'm talking about!" Tommy said furious. "You got Meka on that shit that's why you trying to leave her! You got my cousin hooked nigga!"

Mills looked at Tommy with bug eyes stammering "Man, man listen I…I…. Ain't…She" he said flustered.

He couldn't even form a sentence and Tommy knew he was guilty. He wanted to know why though, why would he do that to his cousin?

"Why?" He inquired hissing through gritted teeth.

It took everything out of Tommy not to pop this nigga in the head right then. His mind continued to wonder and he started trying to rationalize Meka's behavior. He now understood why she had been acting the way she'd been acting. Her hating on Ari and trying to fight her and just the mood swings and attitudes. Tommy knew why his cousin's whole style and personality had changed. The drugs impacted her and altered who she is and who she was.

"Tommy listen …" he stammered.

Tommy couldn't listen and he wouldn't listen. He popped Mills and his body fell limp. Mills slowly began to bleed onto the Lazy Boy. Tommy lifted the strap and pointed it at Cameo. Cameo was QB's boy from his camp and honestly, Tommy at that point didn't trust anybody from his camp or QB's. That's why they were downsizing starting tonight.

"You see anything?" Tommy asked with what he knew was the deadliest look on his face.

"Naw Tommy I ain't seen nothing" he said.

"You got something to say?" He asked looking at Chris.

"Yeah, where we gon' bury him?" he asked.

"I'm sure you and Cameo will figure something out," Tommy turned and walked out.

He didn't have to look back to know that QB was next to him. They hopped into the car and he looked at the time. He saw that Kyra had called but he pushed it to the back of his mind. Now it was time to take care of some real business.

----> More Than a Friend <----

"Strength: the quality or state of being strong"

Chapter 26

Meka couldn't stop crying and shaking. She sat around all the family and her so-called friends. They all were crying, well the ladies were. The men were all straight faced showing no emotion. Someone who she had found herself loving over the past years had been taken from her. Though they'd had their ups and downs, that person had meant a lot to her. She couldn't believe what she had watched on the news earlier. She felt broken, more broken than ever. They'd found her beaten to death and left in the city dam to rot. Two little kids had found her this morning while they played in the restricted area of the park. She was sitting with us all just yesterday. Meka looked at her cousin. He looked so hurt but he wouldn't show it. Meka knew him though better than anyone.

"I can't believe this" She said breaking down again. "We were just together yesterday!"

"I know Meka, I know" Juicy said walking over and wrapping her thick arms around Meka. "Our sister was taken from us and its okay to cry and it's okay to be frustrated" she said rubbing her back.

Meka looked over at Ari who was stone faced. She wasn't crying like the rest of us. She was sitting and looking straight ahead with Tommy's arms wrapped around her. Meka watched the two of them and rolled her eyes. She hated them. She hated *her*. Ari sat with her cousin and he was consoling *her* and not Meka. He cared about *her* tears and not Meka's. Meka looked at her shaking hands and a cool chill ran through her body. She hadn't had a hit in almost six hours and she needed it bad.

"Aye y'all I'm finna be right back" Meka said standing up and everyone looked at her. "What? I'ma run home and come right back."

"Chris ride with her" Tommy instructed without looking at Meka.

"I don't need Chris to ride with me!" she stated and fake lied, "besides, Mills just called me and said he wanted to talk so we gon' talk."

"From now on ain't nobody going anywhere alone. Until I find some loyal bodyguards for everyone we sticking together!" Tommy spoke and looked at Meka waiting for her to say something.

It was his first time looking at her since our incident the night before. She needed to get out. She didn't want Chris seeing her do what she needed to do so badly. She was starting to change, but she knew she had it all under control. Meka was different than most people who shot up; she could stop when she wanted to. Right now, she wanted it to heal the pain of losing Kyra. She'd been there with Meka and Ari from the start, so it was affecting her just as much as the other girls. Meka would stop using in a few weeks after all this was over. She looked at everyone for help, wishing someone would say she was good.

"I'm okay," Meka said turning and Chris turned right behind her. She should have known he would follow after what Tommy demanded.

"You ain't boss, call Uncle Tevin or daddy!" she said with folded arms.

"I don't give a fuck who's boss you can call out! You ain't going anywhere Meka so sit yo ass down!" the tone of his voice let her know he was not up for hearing anything she had to say.

Mad that she didn't bring any soft to hold her over, she sat down trying figure out a way to get exactly what she needed right now. Her hands were shaking and her body temperature had dropped a few degrees, or at least she was shaking like it had.

"You good Meka?" Mia called out. She was looking at her with a raised eyebrow.

"Yeah, I'm good, what the fuck?!" Meka walked out and went to the bathroom. She sat and peed looking up. BINGO!

*****

Everything was flowing through Ari's mind right now. The only person who knew her best other than Tee was gone. How was she going to accept that her friend was murdered? Who would want to murder her, like who? Ari couldn't take it and yet she still couldn't cry. Tee hadn't left her side since this morning when they'd gotten the call. Kyra's brother was the one to reach out to Ari. He'd had to identify the body and he wanted her to be there. He'd had the nerve to say it was Ari's fault Kyra was laying on that cold table. Ari couldn't stomach that. She knew Kyra had been off for the past of couple days, but she just didn't know why.

"I should've known something was up!" Ari said and everyone stared at her. She hadn't noticed that she was speaking out loud the entire time and they were all staring with concerned faces.

"Ari, baby go lay down and get some rest okay?" Tee said and looked at Mia and Juicy. "Yeah sis I'll lay down with you," Mia said walking over to stand Ari up.

"Aye bro, Meka gone" Chris said returning to the living room. "She had to jump out the window" he said and they all jumped up.

"Y'all stay here and don't leave under any circumstances!" Tommy barked. "I'll fuck each and every one of y'all up if y'all leave this house!" he pointed at Mia, Juicy and Ari. "As a matter of fact, Danny ride with us and Justin you stay."

"Aight."

They rushed out and it had Ari's mind spent. What the hell was wrong with Meka that she needed to leave like that? Where the hell was Mills that, he hadn't come over at a time like this? Everything had her mind tripping and she couldn't focus.

*****

Tommy pulled up outside of Meka's and saw her car parked in the drive. He jumped out like a mad man and rushed inside. She was sitting in the living room with her arm still wrapped up in a nod. That fucked him up and he backed away. He had to take a deep breath. His cousin was gone and there wasn't anything he could do about it. He held his tears and walked over to her with Danny next to him.

"Damn dog how long this been going on?" he asked with red puffy eyes.

Tommy had brought him because he knew he was hurt about this Kyra shit and probably wanted to get it off his mind. Danny helped Tommy lift her limp body, slowly pulling the needle out, pulling the band to release it.

"I found out last night" He told him as he wrapped her up in the blanket off her couch.

"Damn this wild," he said helping Tommy get her out to his truck and laying her across the back seat.

Tommy pulled out his phone and called her pops, who answered on the second ring. "What's up son?" he answered in his deep baritone voice.

Tommy didn't know how to say that he'd found his baby girl strung out with a needle in her arm. It didn't look like she had overdosed, but she had something good that was keeping her out for a long time.

"Unc, I just found Meka" He said taking a pause thinking of the right words to say. "She strung Unc, we gotta take her to the hospital."

"What you mean strung?" he asked still too calm for Tommy's liking.

He explained that he'd tried to make her stay with the family and how she jumped out the window. He told him every little detail and he was furious. Tommy didn't want to take her to the hospital knowing they were going to bury Kyra soon.

"Take her now!" his uncle yelled into the phone.

"Okay Unc." Tommy followed his instructions and pulled off to make the drive. He was going to take her to Jefferson Memorial, a drug rehabilitation hospital on the outskirts of the city. It was where all the stars and rich white folks went when they kicked habits. He cut his phone off so he could clear his head.

*****

Damn that was some good dope, Meka thought to herself rolling over. How the hell did I get in my bed? She thought, as she sat up looking around noticing that she wasn't in her bed. She jumped up scared and went to the door and peeped out the small five by five windows. Think Meka, where the fuck did you take your last hit?

Meka started banging on the door and heard somebody yell, "Stop that fuckin' banging bitch we try'na sleep!"

"Where are we?" She screamed out.

"She must be the new girl they brought up in here a few days ago," another chick screamed out. "Baby you at Jefferson."

"OMG would y'all hoes shut the fuck up? I'm try'na get some sleep!" the first girl screamed again.

"I just want to know where I'm at. What is Jefferson? I gotta call my cousin so he can come get me!" Meka screamed out. "Somebody help me!"

"Girl you ain't going nowhere! And the light just came on so you better go to bed and try again in the morning! You keep screaming they gon' sedate you!" she screamed back.

"Who gone sedate me?" for the first time Meka looked down at the band on her wrist and it read 'Jefferson Memorial Drug Rehabilitation'. These mutha-fuckas put me in rehab!

----> More Than a Friend <----

"It's so hard, to say goodbye, to yesterday"

Chapter 27

Ari wasn't prepared for this moment. She took her time slowly getting dressed and quietly sat in the front seat of Tommy's all black on black Bugatti Veyron two-seater. It was a beautiful car and from what she'd heard he dropped a pretty penny on his new toy. When they pulled up they stepped out at the church and it was packed full of people they knew from school and from the hood. Kyra's family was there and none of them would look in Ari's direction. She didn't care, she wasn't the one who did this to her, so how could they blame her? She walked hand-in-hand with Tee as all eyes were on them. She had on a cute black Givenchy midi dress and matching Givenchy stilettos. Her hair was wrapped up in a bun and she rocked a black pair of Gucci sunglasses to cover her face.

Tommy had on a black Gucci pantsuit and Gucci shoes. His hair was neatly pulled back in a low dreaded ponytail and his ears had diamond studs that glistened each time he turned his head. He looked and smelled so good. They marched to a slow beat up to the casket and Ari looked down at her girl. She had on a cheap ass dress that looked like it had come from Wet Seal. She had a pair of fake ass pearls in her ears and a fake ass pearl necklace. It pissed Ari off not to see her go out in style. She deserved to go out wearing a thousand-dollar dress and expensive jewelry just like she did on earth. Danny told the family he had reached out to her family but they didn't want him to take part in anything. They hated on her even in death in Ari's eyes.

Ari pulled off her $20,000 earrings and $10,000 bracelet and started putting them on her. Kyra's sister jumped up and ran over to Ari.

"What are you doing to my sister!" she cried trying to pull Ari away.

"That's **MY** sister!" Ari screamed at her and Tee placed his hand in the middle of her back to calm her. All eyes were locked on the three of them and when Ari looked back to tell Tee to take his hands off her she saw Mia and Juicy standing by her side.

"Y'all got her on all this cheap stuff! *My* sister would *never* be caught *DEAD* in this shit!" Ari screamed meaning every word of what she'd just said and went back to tossing that cheap shit off Kyra and replacing it with her jewelry. "Y'all hating ass mutha-fuckas got her fucked up!"

Everyone had backed off to let Ari finish. She was crying uncontrollably and could barely see through her tears as she did what she knew Kyra would've done for her. When she finished, no one said a word, the entire church was dead silent. All you heard was the song they had replaying of "His Eye is On the Sparrow."

Ari went to take a seat in the third row so she could keep an eye on her jewels and make sure that she was buried with them. She looked to see the PowerPoint that was filled with pictures from her childhood, really old baby pictures, none of how beautiful she had become before she was killed. None with her and any of the people she considered family. They had cropped Ari out of the pictures that she'd been in from their childhood. She was hurt because she'd been there for her when none of them were. The only picture that Ari approved of was a picture of Kyra and her mama. It looked as though they were walking through the park and they stopped to take a picture with her on her mother's hip. They were together again.

"You okay?" Tee asked watching her closely. He himself hadn't said a word to Ari since the walk into the church.

"Yeah I'm good."

He looked at her, not believing what she'd just said.

*****

Tommy took his time searching the crowd for any faces he didn't recognize. He had recently found out that Ari's dad had been contacting Kyra and he think that might have been the person who took her out. He still hadn't told Ari because he wanted the time to be right. He had to get her through this first. Tommy had so much on his plate; searching for his long-lost sister, searching for Ari's dad and Malik, and getting Meka clean, that it had him spread too thin. On top of that, keeping all this from Ari was hurting more than it was helping. He hoped he was making the right decision. He held her hand, keeping her close to him as the whole family exited the church. Tommy scanned the parking lot and spotted a black 94' Cavalier parked. He took out his phone to notify Brown so he could check it out.

"Yeah, it's in the far corner," he said not wanting to look in that direction. "He's here."

Tommy saw Brown emerge from his van and walk briskly to the car and just when he made it over there the car pulled out fast and sped off. He saw his shooter go for his strap but then decided against it. Everyone had looked in his direction and Tommy turned to see Ari burning a hole through him.

"What's going on?" she asked him. Her voice was shaken and she was stuffy from all the crying she'd been doing during the service. For the first time, he noticed that her face looked very plump.

"Not out here" he told her and walked away with her fast on his heels.

"No, who was that? Who was here Tee? Do you know who killed her?"

She flooded him with questions not giving him a chance to answer any of them. Tommy grabbed her and pushed her into the car.

"Not here!" he went around to the driver side of the car and hopped in. He hated to admit it was time to tell her everything, but he didn't know how she was going to take it. She had already been beating herself up, blaming herself for not knowing what had been bothering Kyra. How could I tell her that it was her fault she was dead? I couldn't tell her that Kyra had called me that night, but I was too busy killing somebody to be there for her! Ari was about to blow up and the fire was all on me, he thought waiting for Brown to walk up to his two-seater.

"Tell me Tee!" she screamed her eyes swollen and full of pain.

"Boss man, he fell into the trap! Woody got eyes on him and I'm out to catch him!" Brown stood at his window giving him a report. They had this all planned and now it was time to get it started. Tommy sped out the lot and headed towards his uncle's.

"Take me to the burial site" Ari cried.

"No, you saw her and now you gotta go to Unc's so he can keep you safe while I handle some business."

"No Tee, you will not leave me!" she screamed crying. "Who was there Tee? Who is back?"

"I can't tell you right now just trust me ma!"

"No Tee, tell me baby" she cried and started to hyperventilate. "Who killed my sister Tee? Who took her away from me?"

Tommy couldn't tell her so he ignored her. She started to hit him swinging hard. He parked when he reached his uncle's and hopped out the car. He walked around and pulled her out wrapping his arms tightly around her. She cried and cried and there was nothing he could do to make it better. He held her as she let it out and his mother came out with his uncles and father, watching. Today was the first time he'd seen her cry about it all. She went to his mother and he knew it all had to do with her being broken. Kyra had been there with her through thick and thin. She'd been there when her mom died and when her dad had beat her. She was there even when he wasn't. Tommy had to make this right for Kyra and baby girl. He just had to kill this nigga today and now. His pops knew what it was, he was sure it was written on his face. He followed suit and they all hopped into the van when Brown pulled up and they were off.

----> More Than a Friend <----

"Resilience: the ability to recover from setbacks, adapt well to change, and keep going in the face of adversity; to recover readily after illness or depression"

Chapter 28

Ari's best friend was a thug. It was in his blood. Why did he have to leave me? I needed him and I didn't need to bury him next. Why couldn't he tell me who had done this to my sister? Ari thought to herself, broken and feeling sick to her stomach. She waited until mama left the room and went to the bathroom throwing up nothing but bile. She couldn't remember the last time she'd eaten and started to feel bad. Her baby probably was doing numbers in there starving. She was sure this stress she was feeling wasn't good. She had to remember that she had a little person in her now. She rested her body on the soft, olive green and white comforter, and placed her hand on her belly.

"Hey do you want some soup?" asked Mama as she peeped her head into the room from behind the door. "You know you gotta eat or that son of mine will have both our heads!"

"Come in mama yeah I'm hungry" she walked in with a big bowl of New England clam chowder Ari's favorite. She added clams Ari could tell because there were way more than normal, floating in the hot steaming chowder. She had two pieces of warm biscuits that were buttery and big. Ari's stomach growled and she just stared at it. She had a glass of water with ice cubes on the tray also. Ari took the first biscuit and dragged it through the soup and bit into it. She didn't care it was steaming hot. She wasted no time devouring the bowl until it was empty. Mama sat in a pensive moment before she raised, side eyeing me; not saying a word.

"What?" Ari questioned.

"Nothing" she responded simply.

"Why you staring at me like that?" Ari asked her and she just replied 'mmm' grabbing the tray and walked out. Ari laid back down and placed her hand, softly on her li'l belly. She knew what Mama was thinking, but she wasn't confirming it.

Ari dosed off and woke up to a lot of commotion. When Ari walked outside she saw Tee arguing with some tall girl, wearing a sundress and sandals. She could see the rest of her remaining girls standing there too. They were not too far from the entrance of the driveway. Ari was far enough away, but could still hear everything that was said. She couldn't believe that Meka was locked up in some rehab trying to get off heroine, and Kyra was laid up in her grave. If you would've asked her months ago, where she'd be right now she would had never thought here.

"Man, you better rise up out my brother's face" Juicy said all in the girl's space. Her eyes were still red and swollen like Ari's and the expression on her face was serious and full of hurt and anger.

"Bitch you think I'm scared of you?" the girl said standing a little taller than Juicy.

"I'm not saying be scared, but bitch you better know yo place."

"Juicy chill" Tee said pulling her back.

The girl stood with her girls, still arguing with Tee, it seemed serious as to Ari as she made her way through the crowd. It seemed like everyone had come here after the funeral and they were having a little party for her girl. It made her happy to see so many people showing love. Even though she herself wasn't in the mood.

"Tee, are you ready to leave?" Ari asked walking up to him. She was tired and she wasn't up for any of the partying or bull shit she could see was slowly going to happen in the near future. Unlike everyone else here to show love, she felt broken and alone.

"Yeah come on," he grabbed her hand and they started towards his Bugatti, which wasn't parked far away.

"Oh, you're Ari'Yonna?" The girl exclaimed like she was excited to meet her or like she'd known her for years.

Ari stopped in her tracks and turned to face her and everyone who started to disperse paused to watch.

"Don't fuck with me Davina" Tee warned her as he stared at her with a vehement glare. He got in his "ten toes down" stance as if he was preparing for a battle. Ari wasn't an idiot and it seemed to her like this was one of his hoes and she was probably in her feelings because Ari was staying with him. She'd been nervous about the direction things had been going in with Tee. She really thought that he wanted to be more than friends, but she just couldn't. She still had times she thought about Malik. This washed up, bad replica of Nene Leaks better know that she could have Tee because they were just friends, friends that had sex every now and again.

"Don't even fucking look at her!" he scoffed as he walked Ari to the car, but Davina didn't care. She walked up and tried to swing at Ari, her feelings getting the best of her. She couldn't let Tommy play her, not in front of her girls too.

Ari caught the punch to the chest, weaving so she didn't hit her face. Ari threw a combination of 3 punches landing all. Davina tried to regain her balance but before she could Ari kicked her and she fell completely to the ground. Ari, thankful that mama had made her change clothes into something more comfortable, would've been pissed if she would've fucked up her Givenchy's fucking with one of his bitches.

"Bitch you better know who you fuckin' with!" Ari screamed as Tee pulled her off and pushed her into the car. He secured her, and Davina had gotten up and started to hit

Tee from behind. Losing it, Ari jumped back out but before she could grab her Juicy had her. Justin grabbed both of them apart and ended the fight. Tee grabbed Ari, already knowing her next move and tossed her into the truck rougher than the first time. She sat back, arms folded. Ari wasn't on this at all. She'd just lost her best friend, her sister. Her mind flooded with thoughts about how this was the same reason they'd broken up years ago, because he had hoes trying to fight her at school almost every day. She wasn't feeling this.

"This is why I can't with you Tee," she cried. Ari cried because she cared so much for him but he would never be able to treat her how she felt she should be treated, as his woman, hell as his friend at this point. Yes! He showered her with gifts, love and protection. He had no loyalty in his relationship. He would never be monogamist in their relationship and she couldn't have that. She was hurting. Hurting because she was pregnant by her best friend and she couldn't deal with that. She remembered the first time she'd ever endured one of his other girls. She was sixteen years old and had just had the miscarriage. She was living with Mama and Tee. She wasn't feeling too good because the medicine the doctor had put her on the day before.

I woke up feeling so sick from the medicine Dr. Greene had given me last night. My eyes got teary again. I couldn't believe I had lost my baby. Just the mere thought caused, cramps and I bellowed tumbling over. Tee was still knocked out he must have felt something was wrong because before I knew it he was at my side.

"What's wrong Ari?" he asked attempting to lift me up. He picked my whole body up without uncurling me.

"My stomach still hurts," I cried. It was everything though. It was the thought of my daughter. It was the fact my father had beaten the baby out of me. I had no one just Tee and Mama. I cried and he held me. I finally managed to get myself together when I heard my best friend Kyra calling my name. I wondered down the steps and the rest of our friends were there. We sat on the porch for most of the day when a group of girls walked up on us. Tee must have known the girls because he instantly jumped up.

"Tommy where the fuck you been at? Why you ain't answerin' none of my fuckin' calls?" One girl with red long weave said. She had really long finger nails and a really big butt. She wasn't ugly either. She was too dark for that color hair if you asked me. Whoever put it in did a terrible job and you could tell she thought she was show stopping.

"Monifa I told you 'bout comin' round here without callin' da fuck wrong wit' you?" he yelled while taking quick glances in my direction.

It didn't take me long to put two-and-two together. He was dating this girl too. Here I am mourning the loss of our baby and he's fucking around with other girls. I stood up and turned to go in the house. I heard him yelling *and fussing. I had just brought my bag in so it was still neatly piled in the corner. I grabbed it and walked out the house. He tried to chase me and I screamed for him to just stop. We had been together officially for 2-years and that's how he was treating me. I thought that was the end of me and Tee, but that just led to something that locked us in forever.*

Ari pulled up to the hotel and she hopped out. Tee pulled off and just like that she was alone. They hadn't spoken the whole ride home, besides her cries. She looked into the mirror and at her belly. She remembered this just like before. The only difference was she wasn't that pregnant, abused, 16-year old girl with nowhere to go and no money. She didn't want her baby to be torn between two broken homes. She'd heard her cell blazing, and looked and saw it was Kyra's number. Her heart fluttered and she fell back onto the bed.

Without waiting any longer, she answered, "Hello".

"Ari'Yonna" a deep voice spoke through the phone.

She knew that voice and knew what was happening. She knew everything. Ari couldn't take it. She dropped the phone and packed up as much as she could get to fit into her car, left a note and jumped on the road. She drove and drove for a few hours with no direction, when she heard her tire pop. It was 12 in the morning and she was stranded on the side of the road. Ari couldn't call anyone from what she now considered her past. She had no family, they were Tee's family. She had no friends, they were

Tee's friends. Only person she had was Kyra and now she no longer had her. She no longer had anyone. She was alone, really alone and now she'd have to start over. She had to start over because the little one in her stomach was depending on her. She didn't want to raise her child in this environment. She wanted her baby to have a different life, one that didn't include taking others' lives. She wanted her child to have a choice on how it wanted to live and the direction it wanted to go in.

There was only one direction that T.A.A went in and she didn't want that for her baby.

Ari placed her head in her hands letting it all out again. She had invested so much energy into other people and what they felt she should do, but now she wanted to live. She didn't want that for herself anymore. She no longer wanted to exist in this dangerous world, she wanted to live. She deserved to live. She deserved to live because Kyra couldn't. She deserved to live because her mother couldn't. Everyone Ari loves dies and she couldn't stomach the thought of anyone else dying because of her. They all deserved to live and that's exactly what she'd planned to do. She'd planned to live for her and hers, she thought rubbing her belly. She had to take a leap of faith and get as far away from T.A.A as she possibly could. She had to because her life depended on it. Her unborn child's life depended on it. This life was toxic and she had to do whatever it takes to exist, to *live* without it. She screamed, and no one could hear her. She was alone and stranded and she had nowhere to go. She heard a knock on the window, "You need some help?"

"I'm okay," she responded nervously. There stood a tall fine ass man with dreads that barely reached his shoulders. He had a nicely trimmed beard and he had distinct brown eyes.

"No, you're not, my name Wayne ma how can I help?"

----> More Than a Friend <----

Prolepsis

I stepped off the plane back to business. I had finally gotten things in order with my family and now to start the summer off good I had planned a Memorial Day ball for all the fallen soldiers. A lot had changed and I was ready for everything else to fall into place. I was the man, QB my right hand and everything was how it was supposed to be. At least to me that's how it seemed. I got into the back seat of the black Tahoe with two of my most trusted body guards. I linked hands with my leading lady knowing this was exactly what I had been yearning for over the past few years. When Ari left me it hurt me to my core and turned me cold-blooded. I was my father's child. So many people had lost their lives, families and positions. Ari leaving me was a wakeup call that I needed to change and it took a while for me to be the man I was today. Now I was able to be the man I needed to be for this lovely lady sitting next to me. I kissed her hand as we pulled off into traffic. Picking up my phone I called QB to make sure everything was everything with the camps.

"Yeah, my team and I will arrive a little later than you and your team, but we all will be in attendance" he answered taking a drag from what he was smoking.

"Alright brother" I clicked and looked at my beautiful bride-to-be. We pulled up to our home and got right to business. She started gathering our necessities and laying out our attire for the night. We had maybe two hours to get dressed.

"So, is QB finally bringing one of his girls tonight?" my bride-to-be asked while slipping into her custom Vera Wang gown we had purchased in Punta Cuna. It fit her curves so well. She had gained so much weight over the past few weeks and wore it well. I couldn't help but to stare and imagine myself behind her, looking down with my hand placed on her perfectly arched back, while she tossed her ass back and made it clap on my dick at the same time. My dick was definitely at full attention and she stared at me with her perfectly manicured French tips placed on her hip and tight lips.

"Excuse me" she said looking down and I knew she was thinking the same thing or something close. "Save that for tonight."

She walked into our closet and pulled out a shoe box. "You were right! These shoes go perfectly with this dress!" She was excited and I was happy for her. She had been through so much over the past few months and I was grateful to see her smile and hear her giggles.

We dressed quickly and headed out to the ball. As we pulled up I checked out the crowd and noticed that everyone we knew was there. I had brought the whole city and surrounding cities out to celebrate the death of our lost ones and to also celebrate life. The life that we were all still blessed to have. For six-months straight our streets had to be "cleaned" up. Too many people we fucked with talked to people they shouldn't have been talking to and too many people schemed on people they shouldn't have tried to scheme on. When the time comes that people want to try loyalty and greatness, you have to make sure you on the winning team.

  I grabbed a glass of champagne for my leading lady and guided her over to our section. We had each section separated and reserved for our camps. There were tables spread around for the common folk who loved and worshiped T.A.A. The hall was decorated and designed by my love. She had sat down with a team of professionals, designed the layout and they made it come true. I loved to see her vision brought to life. She had a niche for design and that was one thing I loved about her on top of everything else.

  We sipped our champagne and talked with our closest friends and family. We'd come a long way and the people that we had left, that managed to survive the hardest times with us were here. Honestly, I had certain feelings now towards everyone I loved and trusted. My motto would never change, cliché or not, to keep your family close and your enemies closer til' they died, one or the other. I pulled Baby into me and kissed her. I missed this so much and was so happy that everything was finally how it should be. I was happy.

  I looked up when I saw everyone's attention turn towards the door. I saw my brother first and the pretty lady he had on his arms. I think for the first time ever in life my heart skipped a beat. I could see her from afar. She was beautiful. Her features stood out and I couldn't help but to be wrapped in her beauty. I never thought this day would come after searching for so many years. Every search ended with the same results, nothing. I had searched long and hard to find her and there she stood with her arms interlocked with my right-hand man, my brother. QB meant more to me than a lot of men I called brothers or cousins, and there he stood with this beauty, his hand now resting upon her small waist.

I slowly approached with my woman by my side. She had sandy brown hair that fell right below her shoulder blades. She had a caramel complexion like mine. She was really thick, I noticed even though I didn't want to. She was short, only looking to stand at about 5'2'. Her eyes were brown and had a circle of a lighter brown color, like my eyes. She had long eyelashes and had the prettiest teeth I had ever seen. She was gorgeous. She looked just like me, and from this moment on I knew that I had to be there for her. We were one and the same. She was my sista.

*****

I couldn't stop staring at her and now everyone around us was staring, I'm sure they were all thinking the same thing. It took a young up and coming gangsta in QB's camp to break the silence.

"Damn, y'all look just alike, are y'all related?" Goldee said with the most confused look on his face.

He was a young goon trying to come up and I respected that. That's why I placed him in QB's camp after having that "talk" with Goldee to protect my brother with his life, no matter what.

"What's ya name shorty?" I asked her.

She paused and looked at QB before answering. "TaMera Mi'Lady Samuels," she answered in a modulated tone that caused me to smile. It seemed like we were the only two in that moment. "What's your name?" she asked and I knew then that she was educated.

She seemed smart, at least that's the vibe I was getting from the way she carried herself. In that moment, my mind drifted off thinking of Ari. She reminded me of Ari so much. She was beautiful, soft-spoken and educated, like me. I was a gangsta no doubt, but I was also smart and well educated. I had gotten good grades in school and had graduated in the top ten of my class. There was no dummy in me at all and I could tell it ran in the family.

"I'm Thomas, everybody calls me Tommy" I said not able to hold my words any longer. "You're my sister." I pulled her into a hug and her body stiffened. "My uncle told me a lot about you."

She stood quietly taking everything in and trying to figure things out. I didn't know what she was thinking, and she didn't show any emotion whatsoever.

"I've been searching ever since I heard about your mom's and everything."

"Y'all do look just alike" Cameo, QB's front runner of his camp added.

He was looking at us back and forth like he couldn't believe it himself. He dapped me up, giving me the most gangsta handshake, and wrapped his arms around a dark brown-skinned girl's waist. She must be Shatia. I had heard a lot about her, being that she was protected by T.A.A. because she was his girl, but I'd never met her personally. I didn't like what I'd heard; mostly that she was loud, ghetto and always in some shit. But I trusted QB and his ratchet camp. He thought highly of them and I couldn't say anything because I trusted him.

"What's up?" Keno walked up and grabbed TaMera's arm.

I frowned instantly and I could tell she wasn't feeling it either because she seemed nervous and shaken up. I looked at my brother for some type of sign to let me know what was up with Keno and why he was grabbing on shorty like that. The look on his face said everything I needed to hear.

"Ummm hey," she said not really seeming like she wanted to be touched.

"So, you back with this nigga?" he said pointing to QB who was just standing there watching everything unfold. I knew my brother and knew he was seconds away from knocking this nigga out.

Keno was a cool nigga for the most part and wise with money. He was a team eastside nigga, up in New York that worked with Wayne for a while. He handled shit and researched shit that ended up helping me out a lot. What I didn't like was how he was coming after QB and my sister right now.

"Not right now Keno," she said giving him a little push to put some space in between them.

"Actually, partna we over here having a little family discussion, so I'ma need you to back up aight?" I stepped in trying to defuse a situation that I saw unfolding.

I didn't want any drama at this event my lady had worked so hard to put together. Especially after the hard few months that had passed us. Secondly, I needed to get more info on the circle of people I had around me, starting with miss TaMera. My bad, miss Lady.

"Actually, here is my card" I handed her a business card from my realtor company. "It got my number on it and QB knows where I stay." I watched her just stare at the card for a minute before she said thanks and was pulled away by her girls. I turned to see my beautiful soon-to-be wife walking towards the table with champagne. I turned to QB after dismissing the niggas left standing around us, including my guards.

"My brother this whole time she's been under my nose" I said still hardly believing it.

"Why you ain't tell me what was up? We brothers" he said sounding hurt and confused.

"I mean I only just found out and I searched but never came up with no leads!" I tried to explain to him.

I shook my head and realized that our family had lied to us both. His mom knew and didn't say anything either. I stood for ten minutes giving him the breakdown on everything that I knew he didn't know. He had no idea that the woman I had searched for so many years was under my watch and my care the whole time. So many years had passed and she had been under my nose since day one. If this nigga wasn't so private, we would have been known. I looked forward to our meeting tomorrow and I had every intention on bringing this family back together. Whether my father was with it or not.

Made in the USA
Columbia, SC
13 July 2019